A Spoonful of Gunpowder

Katherine H. Brown

A Spoonful of Gunpowder

ISBN: 979-8-9867030-2-2

Copyright © 2022 by Katherine Brown

All rights reserved.

This book or any portion thereof may not be reproduced or used in any manner whatsoever without the express written permission of the publisher except for the use of brief quotations in a book review.

Portions of this book are works of fiction. Any references to historical events, real people, or real places are used fictitiously. Other names, characters, places and events are products of the author's imagination, and any resemblances to actual events or places or persons, living or dead, is entirely coincidental.

Book design by Katherine Brown Books

First Printing, 2022

www.katherinebrownbooks.com

Acknowledgements

This book is brought to you in part by playdough, naptime, and my mother, Della. Each of these occupied my toddler for long periods of time and are the only reason I got any writing accomplished at all.

I'm also grateful to my sister for always being an excellent sounding board as I bounce ideas around and to my husband for never questioning why I need to get new or different bookmarks printed.

Chapter One

It was easy to skirt around the ticket agent. He was fast asleep at his post these early pre-dawn hours. The sentries circling in front and behind the one and only lift to the airship tower several stories above ground would have been more difficult if she hadn't helped Uncle Ernest create them. Anna-Marie hid behind a stout post until the first iron automaton rolled past, then quick as lightning darted out and stuck a copper filigreed key into the clockwork mechanism below the left hip of the machine. A hard turn of the key to the left and the guard went still, the treads upon which it rolled jerking to a halt. The spherical red eyes dimmed. Both arms relaxed to the side of the automaton's bulky body with a whir and a hiss as the miniature steam engine inside cooled down, the water blocked from entering the chamber that heated and powered the weapons located in each metal finger.

Less than a minute later, she disabled the second sentry the same way before slipping onto the waiting lift.

Did she have the money to buy a ticket? Of course. But as she didn't plan to come back to this place once she was away, she saw no point in spending perfectly good money that would simply find its way back to Uncle Ernest's fat pockets. Everything in this seaside town was run by Uncle, even if the villagers didn't realize it.

As she threw the lever and let herself be carried into the night sky by the cables of the lift, she laughed. He would be angry when he found the sentries disabled.

The dock itself wasn't large or impressive. The only reason it had sentries or a ticket agent in the first place was because Uncle Ernest built the dock and made the rules. He wanted his precious shipments protected. She clenched her teeth and turned her back resolutely on the lift and the town. There was one ship docked and lucky for her, it didn't appear to have a bustling crew to spot her as she shimmied across a rope agile as a monkey and dropped onto the deck behind coils of ropes and stacks of buckets.

Hours later, Anna-Marie bit back an exclamation as the airship hit a blast of turbulence causing a crate of oranges to fall, barely missing her foot. She scooted further into the corner of the storage hold as the sound of footfalls warned her someone was coming.

Her hand came into contact with a tarpaulin covering a stack of cargo. Slowly, she inched it out of place and over herself.

For several minutes, only footsteps, the sound of rolling fruit, and muttered curses broke the silence.

The airship swayed gently but it was enough to scatter oranges in every direction again. One bumped her foot through the tarpaulin. She squeezed her eyes shut.

"Come here, you," a man muttered.

Anna-Marie watched through a tiny hole in the tarp as the man drew right up next to her. She hardly dared to breathe as he bent down. She braced herself for him to discover her hiding place then felt the tap against her leg as he grabbed the wayward orange.

"Got you." He stood, tossing his prize into the crate.

And then the unthinkable happened. The ship veered into a sharp turn and every single orange still on the floor rolled toward her and subsequently beneath the man's feet. Through the slit in her covering, she could make out one of his arms flailing as he yelped and then he fell, crashing right into her.

"Oomph!" She couldn't stop the grunt as she took his weight in her midsection.

For his part, the man ripped the tarpaulin from her head in surprise but made no move to get up. "What have we here? A stowaway?"

"Please, don't tell the captain. My uncle begged me to go to London for him." *Ordered.* "He needs me to see to his affairs." *True.* She worked up a sniffle and held a gray handkerchief in front of her face. "He's an invalid." *True, even if he is no less capable than the average, no, above-average, individual.* Anna-Marie pinched her mouth and hunched her shoulders, making herself look frightened and hopefully pitiful enough to leave alone. It would be such an inconvenience to be tossed from an airship so far from her destination.

The man seemed to consider this plea, though Anna-Marie had trouble reading his face in the shadows and dim light thrown into the cargo hold from one small port window. She held herself still, though the temptation to shove the man off and find a weapon was strong. A broken board from the crate lid looked particularly effective, if she could get untangled and free herself from this position, she would have no lack of options within easier reach. Even now she could feel the hilt of the blade in her sleeve digging into her forearm as if begging to be unsheathed.

At last, the man spoke though he remained on top of her. "Such a polite stowaway. And why would I keep your secret?"

His voice had a musical quality like that of laughter. In fact, from the flash of white teeth she could just make out a wide grin, but she perceived no threat in it. Still, she narrowed her eyes. "I shall make you a deal. If you keep my secret and keep anyone else from coming down here to discover me, I shall collect all of the overturned cargo and put everything back in place. You won't have to step another foot in the hold."

"Maybe I like it in the hold." His lopsided grin was evident for certain as he leaned closer to peer at her. "Infinitely better company down here."

"Oh, for the love of tea and biscuits! Get off." Anna-Marie had had it. Just as she inhaled, gathering all her strength to remove the annoying man from her person, a yell sounded from above.

The man sighed before standing to his feet. "I best see what all the ruckus is about. Probably the boiler acting up again."

Much to Anna-Marie's surprise, he held out a hand and gently lifted her to her feet. "I didn't catch your name."

"I didn't offer it."

He studied her a second longer and then gave a nod. "Alright then. Put all the cargo to rights. Except the oranges. You can chuck the bloody oranges out the window for all I care." With a wink and a grin, he spun on his heel and left her staring as he crossed the hold and bounded up the steps to the deck above.

Anna-Marie did not think of that gorgeous grin as she straightened crates and barrels. She did not shake her head and bite back a smile when she collected all of the oranges, indeed considering chucking the troublesome fruits out into the sky. And her breath certainly did not catch in anticipation as footsteps sounded on the steps sometime later as she lounged on a bag of flour eating one of the oranges.

That is what she told herself anyway. Shaking away her amusement, Anna-Marie shifted her grip on the knife in her hand, ready to throw it at the newcomer if necessary.

"I see my gallant act of bringing you food and water to assure you didn't starve were unnecessary." The man from before held up a beaker and what looked like an end of crusty bread.

She could see him better as he stood on the steps, that teasing smile firmly in place. He had sandy hair, windblown and sticking up in various directions that made her fingers itch to brush it back down. He wore tall boots, a loose white shirt and tan breeches. He was neither large nor thin. His expression of mirth and light-hearted manner set him apart from any other men she knew but it also made her nervous. She couldn't predict him.

"Thank you," she managed to say as he brought the food. She held up a sliver of orange in a truce and he accepted. "What was wrong with the boiler?"

"Hmm? Oh. Isn't staying hot enough. We have lost quite a bit of altitude. That is why the ship keeps changing course, I'm told, to catch the power of the wind with the emergency sail as the balloon is less than reliable at the moment."

"You'll need to insulate the boiler." Anna-Marie spoke the words without thought and cringed inwardly. Poor, unassuming women should not talk of engineering or mechanics.

"You think so?" He chewed on his orange thoughtfully, as if he didn't notice her blunder. "How would one do that?"

She shrugged. "It depends on the boiler. I suppose you could wrap it with a wool blanket for a time; however you might instead look into the new method of using steel instead of iron for boilers. I've heard a man by the name of Kelly in the Americas is creating batches and batches of them. 'Tis only a matter of time before plants begin producing it in factories throughout the cities here."

For a moment, he stared at her with his mouth wide. To Anna-Marie's surprise, he didn't look offended or doubtful of her words. Before she could determine what his thoughts were exactly on a woman lecturing him on boilers and metals and such, another shout arose on deck.

This time, it was a different cry, "London, ho!"

"I have to be going," Anna-Marie said hastily. As she stood, she flicked her skirts to cover her no-nonsense red ankle boots that boasted spikes protruding front and back from the toes and heels. "Good luck with the boiler." And without waiting for a reply, she hopped from crate to crate and to the bottom step before disappearing upward.

If she had glanced back, Anna-Marie would have been flabbergasted to see the widest smile yet as the man chuckled and shook his head, never taking his eyes off of her retreating figure.

Chapter Two

After her hasty departure from the airship, Anna-Marie strolled through the city, observing the lack of young ladies out on their own and even the diminished number of orphans on the street in the poor areas as she made her way to the first destination she had in mind. Number Thirteen Cherry Blossom Lane.

If someone wanted to find Cherry Blossom Lane, all they would have to do is ask the policebot stationed outside the railway platform. Dubbed "coppers" for the copper makeup of their exterior that houses the numerous pistons and gears operated by a condensate recycling boiler, the small but efficient army of policebots are spread out at stations near each major intersection. The copper will undoubtedly whiz and whir, perhaps emit a bit of steam, then spit out a small list of steps on a thin white card.

Despite the tiny print and unimaginative directions-two rights, a left, and a sharp right again sure enough, you're there—right in the middle of Cherry Blossom Lane. Anna-Marie felt it would have been more accurate and better warning to word the directions thus: walk until the street sweeper automatons have drawn a line in the cobblestone they refuse to cross, turn right at the pile of garbage, right again at the burnt-out chapel, a left at the rookery, and a sharp right when the sounds of steam vehicles is so far behind you that you are no longer sure they exist.

If the dull copper had a modicum of human intelligence, rather than the simple programming codes by which he functions, he would probably avoid giving you the directions. Instead, he would likely warn you to stay far, far away from Cherry Blossom Lane, especially Number Thirteen.

Anna-Marie Pauper, however, did not stop to ask the policebot for directions. Anna-Marie Pauper knew exactly how to get to Number Thirteen, Cherry Blossom Lane. Her own surname was courtesy of the establishment found at that address, after all. Rather than approaching immediately, Anna-Marie spent half an hour observing the house. Not a curtain flicked nor a soul stirred in the windows. After ten such tedious minutes, she snuck into the kitchen. Empty. Seeing the ashes had not yet been collected from the ash box, she caught sight of a paper poking through them. She sifted through the box with her umbrella, uncovering many such scraps that had escaped burning other than a portion here and there. She reached into her pocket and extracted a tin of wax, melting it with the heat of her hands and using it to piece the page together. What she read made her smile as her brain whirred with a new plan even as she wondered which of the girls had written the desperate, misspelled plea for a savior.

Her tall red boots shuffled softly on the cobblestones as she stopped in front of the gray-brick building, approaching from the end of the lane as if she hadn't already been sneaking around inside. The cracked foundation bespoke its age and a new layer of mold decorated the base of the steps. Only one iron railing remained and the paint was chipping off of the once elegant scrollwork of lilies. She didn't take much notice of the poor state of upkeep; it had looked just as sad and defeated when she had lived there as a girl. Behind her, the street was quiet, except for the steady clopping hooves of a weathered old nag pulling a dilapidated cart of bruised apples. Refuse filled the gutters lending an aroma that made one breathe through their mouth rather than nose. The fancy new steam carriages and autos didn't pass down Cherry Blossom Lane, not if they could help it. Potholes large enough to swallow a small dog marked the narrow way, some were still full of water from a recent rain. Even hackney cabs charged double the fee to traverse Cherry Blossom Lane.

With one hand, she snapped her large—obscenely large, some would say—gray lace and red leather umbrella shut with a click. She then peeled the supple, brown leather gloves from her fingers and stuffed them in her carpet bag, taking it in the other hand. After straightening her pert red hat and giving a tug to her leather corset, Anna-Marie climbed the steps and gave three sharp raps on the door with the tip of her umbrella.

Located at Number Thirteen was the Pauper House for Girls, an orphanage owned by one Mr. Lucifer Banks. Mr. Banks was a villain of the worst sort—a wealthy aristocrat, miserly in excess, who refused to spend a tuppence on the upkeep of the orphanage or its inhabitants. The man only stepped foot in the orphanage each year at Christmas for a token newspaper interview about his contributions to the poor.

She remembered the first year she lived in the orphan house, a small child of four, and the fierce scrubbing all of the children were given in a bath with coal tar soap that left the skin red for hours. They were made to beat all of the rugs and wipe the front hall to a shine. Anna-Marie particularly remembered a pair of brushes being tied to her hands and knees with scraps of old linens and being told to crawl over the whole floor until it was clean. She imagined the great man who was coming to see them, the man who all of that cleaning and work was done for, must be wonderful to deserve such a welcome. Lucifer Banks barged into the orphan house and his countenance was so harsh that she was stricken immobile with fear. Even when he yelled at her to move out of his way, she hadn't been able to. The devil had pushed her aside with the toe of his boot as if touching her pained him.

The nursemaid, for at the time a few of the staff had still remained to care for the smallest children, had approached Mr. Banks and mentioned the need for a new crib. He refused saying that to be discontent was a sin and the urchins should learn to share. Being four, Anna-Marie hadn't been able to count very high yet but she knew that at least three babes shared a drawer for a bed, removed from a dresser that was in the trash heap. Two of the babies suffocated within a week.

Each year for the next twelve years that she resided at the orphan house, he came and the fuss and preparation were the same. As she got older, Anna-Marie realized the cleaning and airing had more to do with Lucifer Banks having his interview and likeness in the paper than with any actual preference for how the orphan house, or the orphans, looked. He never lingered once his adoring public vacated the building.

The door opened promptly, summoning Anna-Marie back to the present, and her first view was of a familiar figure.

"Good afternoon, Constantina."

Barely four feet tall and half as round, the rudimentary automaton in front of her opened the door wider. "Miss Pauper. I'll gather the tea things." An apron tied around her neck and midsection was losing its frills but gave indication that she was a maid. The automaton did not have feet but glided on a small platform base instead.

Anna-Marie might have smiled, proud the programming she installed during her youth was still within the domestic little machine, if she weren't there on such an important errand. "I'm afraid tea will have to wait. Please hold my bag." She let herself in the door, moving around Constantina with the ease of someone who had done so many times before, while simultaneously depositing a drab carpet bag on the outstretched metal arm. "Is the master in the study?"

Of course, he was in the study. He was always in the study. The only place where he spent a greater amount of time than the study was in his cups.

Not pausing for a moment, she marched down the hall, relishing the clomp of her boots on the scarred and bowed hardwood floors, and let herself into the dark room. "Godfrey Letchford."

The grizzled old man in the creaking wooden chair behind the desk let out a groan before tossing back the last swallow of cheap liquor and pouring another glass. "Little Anna-Marie Pauper. What bloody nightmare is this, to have the likes of your scrawny self returned to my doorstep?"

"Lovely to see you, as always." Anna-Marie ran a gloved finger across the arm of a chair. A thick layer of dust danced at the disturbance. It was difficult to see the grime beneath the dust, but the disgustingly thick layers were there, same as they'd been five years ago. She chose to remain standing—not that she'd been invited to sit anyway-as she couldn't imagine what vermin might have taken up residence in the large hole torn in the cushion of the only other chair. "Fortunately for the both of us, Godfrey, this is not a social visit. I'm here to answer the advertisement."

"The what?"

Anna-Marie sighed. Godfrey wasn't the quickest cog…well, ever…but even less so by afternoon when he was at least two bottles in for the day. She would have to spell it out for him.

Anna-Marie reached into one of numerous front pockets on her long blue overcoat, extracting the soot-streaked piece of paper she had so recently discovered and mended, unfolding it gingerly. She read aloud: "Wanted: New overseer for Pauper House for Girls. Requirements for position include sober disposition, rosy cheeks, no metal parts. Must be female, smart, and not too stingy. No more gruel. Please come soon or sooner. Apply in person, Thirteen Cherry Blossom Lane." She skipped over the poor spelling, reading the soot-stained paper with a little more flair than it had probably been written with. Through her tone and determined expression, she hoped to convey confidence and disdain at once. *'Act like you belong and so you shall'*, another life lesson from Uncle Ernest. Now that she had decided to get rid of Godfrey for the sake of whichever girls remained here, she wouldn't be put off, least of all by the worthless drunk himself.

As she read from the paper, Godfrey Letchford's face had colored to the shade of an overripe tomato. He was spluttering mad as Anna-Marie calmly refolded the paper and returned it safely to its place.

"Now…" She gave a tap of the umbrella on the wooden floor. "I believe you're in my study. I'll have to ask you to leave." As she said the words, Anna-Marie hung her overcoat on the drooping hat stand, a bit surprised it didn't immediately fall over with the added weight.

"Leave? You've lost your marbles."

"I assure you, I never lose anything, not even marbles. I believe we can agree that I fit the bill exactly. Now, I've come to accept the position as overseer. Good day." Though she prided herself on good manners, she couldn't find it inside herself to add the word *sir*.

Godfrey's chair clattered to the floor as he roared upright. "I am the only overseer of this place, and you're nothing but an orphan chit with too much attitude and not enough beatings." He stomped around the desk, raising a hand as if to strike.

Three things happened in very quick succession.

First, Anna-Marie raised her umbrella, blocking the downward swing of Godfrey's arm and using his own momentum to spin and propel the man toward the door.

Second, the closed door swung open. The heavyset Godfrey was sent sprawling through it, landing none too lightly on his back with a grunt.

Last, a dirty black boot kicked out at Godfrey's head. Attached to the boot, a tall and lanky young man tipped his hat.

"Been wanting to do that most of me life." He grinned, his accent coarse but his voice positively chipper. "Good afternoon, sweet Anna-Marie. I heard you were back and couldn't resist seeing for myself." The man leaned against the door jamb, hooking his thumbs into his gray suspenders and eyed her slowly from head to spiked boots where his gaze widened a fraction.

Anna-Marie, neither surprised nor perturbed at the audacity of such a look, merely nodded at the tall man, familiar but changed. Grown. The harsh planes of his cheeks gave him a more hardened appearance than she remembered but she spoke casually to the old friend she hoped still remained beneath. "Ah, Norbert. You're just in time to help me take out the rubbish."

A cheer went up from the landing at the top of the narrow staircase.

At that same moment, Constantina rolled into the hallway. "Tea is served. Tea is served. Tea is served." Unable to go around the lump that was Godfrey's unconscious form sprawled across the floor, the automaton thumped against it repeatedly, causing quite the clatter to the dishes atop the varnished silver tea tray clasped in her metal hands.

"I'll take that, thank you." Anna-Marie rescued the tray posthaste. If the cracked tea set were to get one more chip, it would be in danger of no longer being able to hold the tea.

Relieved of her burden, Constantina's inner mechanisms whirred; cogs whined as they turned slowly. The brass figure, shaped very much like a pear, returned to her docking station in the foyer.

"We'll get you some fresh oil soon," Anna-Marie murmured after her.

~

Having secured a promise from Norbert that Godfrey would be removed far, far away from the orphanage, Anna-Marie attended to the next matter of business.

Tea.

"Where are the others?" As she poured the steaming cups, she looked at the four girls sitting and slouching before her.

"It's only us."

"Only four?"

A slim girl of about twelve, with honey-colored hair in two braids, nodded. "The rest are gone. Vanished."

"Quiet, Tempy." A kick from one of the three older girls silenced the younger one.

"You must be Temperance," Anna-Marie said, handing the young girl a teacup.

"Yes."

"And you three, I remember. Patience, Prudence. Vivien."

Vivien, whose downturned mouth and narrowed eyes gave no doubt of her desire to kick Anna-Marie as well, said, "Yes. So very kind of you to remember us, Anna-Marie. To what do we owe this little visit after five years without a word or backward glance?"

Anna-Marie stiffened. "I've come to help."

"You abandoned us," Viven said, her voice thick with ire. She flipped her dark brown curls over her shoulder. "We don't want your help."

Each of the girls taken in by Pauper House were given the same last name—Pauper. Thus they became their own ragtag little family. Infants were even given first names, just as Prudence and Patience had been, if they survived past the age of one. As the oldest, Anna-Marie had been the first to leave their little family. She sighed.

"I understand why you see it that way. However, like it or not, you not only need my help, but you also want it. Otherwise, there would have been no advertisement requesting a new overseer, now would there?"

"Advertisement?" Viven snapped curtly.

Next to her, a freckle-faced young lady's mouth dropped open. She snapped it shut immediately. Her auburn hair was twisted into a bun at the nape of her neck, and she tucked imaginary strands in place as she looked down at her feet.

"Prudence?" Vivien pressed with a hiss.

Each of the freckles disappeared beneath the flush rising to her cheeks. "I tore it up and threw it in the fire, just like you said. Honest, Vivien." She shuffled her feet. Or, I tossed it into the ash box at least. I didn't take it to the paper to print, I swear. Didn't have the money to do it anyway," she muttered.

"Come, come. How I received the advertisement is not important." Anna-Marie bit back a smile, glad to have discovered the author of the witty but heartfelt plea for a new overseer, finished handing around the tea, then sat on a lumpy settee. And regretted it. Standing would have been more comfortable, though perhaps a little unorthodox while one was drinking tea. With a sigh, she continued speaking from her uncomfortable perch on the ancient piece of furniture. "You three are all about to reach your majority. You haven't been adopted. Tell me, if you don't need my help, what are your plans for your future after you turn seventeen and are turned out onto the street?"

"A governess, maybe?" Prudence answered, shying away from Vivien's angry glance.

"Or we can do mending. Some ladies earn respectable wages mending and darning." Patience, her twin by birth, favored Prudence in hair color alone. Her complexion was clear, not a freckle in sight. Patience's green eyes were smaller than her sister's blue ones, and her skin was darker, as if she spent more time in the sun.

"Oh, good. You've all acquired the proper skills for such posts, then?" Anna-Marie pierced them each with a long look. "It seems to me a governess might be expected to spell accurately in order to teach spelling to any pupils. And you are familiar with classic literature? Proper etiquette? The finer stitches and needlepoint arts?"

The girls squirmed. Vivien crossed her arms over her chest, the motion stretching the threadbare sleeves to the point of tearing at the shoulder.

"Precisely as I thought. You are no more prepared to go your own way than I was. You'll be matchstick girls if you're lucky; women of the night if you aren't. No, it will never do to leave you on your own. Not to mention, we have the apparent disappearances of girls from the neighborhood to think of. Clearly, we have much to do." Anna-Marie took a bracing sip of tea, then settled the cup in a saucer on the table. "Now, I shall make up a list of chores for each of you. You'll find them on your beds in a quarter of an hour. I expect everyone to hop to it as soon as you've finished your tea."

Vivien jumped to her feet, eyes blazing. "You think you can swoop down in here and start bossing us around now that you have nice clothes and some fancy way of talking? Well, you're wrong. We don't have to listen to the likes of you, and there's not a thing you can do about it." She stormed from the room.

Anna-Marie listened to the girl's stomping feet ascend the stairs and clucked her tongue. "If there are no other arguments, I shall be off to buy some lubricants for Constantina, as well as some decent food. Don't worry—no gruel." With a wink at Prudence, she stood. Behind her back, she slipped a small hair comb into the cushion, pushing it just far enough down that it would not likely be noticed.

Three sets of eyes watched in awe as she glided from the room, elegant neck long, back straight, and chin up.

The moment she stepped out of the parlor, excited chatter broke out among the girls.

"I can't believe she's back."

"She was a girl here? When did she leave?"

"Nobody could torment old Godfrey like Anna-Marie Pauper. Of course, he deserved it. Mean as the dickens when he ran out of whiskey."

Not waiting to hear the rest, Anna-Marie let herself out.

Chapter Three

Anna-Marie drew herself onto the front steps and took a deep breath. The thick, damp fog was not refreshing. She ignored her disappointment at Vivien's reaction, should have expected it, truly. The girl had always been haughty, considered herself above Anna-Marie and the other orphans, who had been abandoned in the streets at birth, simply because she had arrived as an older child after the death of her parents. Vivien had once been wanted, loved, and she never got used to being discarded after her parents died. She had set out to make all the others pay for her pain from when that love disappeared.

Being several years her senior, not to mention cocky in her own respect, Anna-Marie had brushed off the young girl's venomous attitude, assuming the tyrant of a child would one day grow up. She had grown up, all right, into a vindictive, bitter young woman, from the looks of it.

A glance at one dirty second-floor window revealed a scowling face quickly concealed by the flick of a shabby curtain. Anna-Marie pursed her lips and turned back to the street.

She would deal with Vivien later.

Right now, she had work to do.

She opened her umbrella beneath the dry sky. Umbrellas, Anna-Marie thought, were one of life's most underrated articles. They kept the rain off, the sun at bay, hid your face when needed, and could easily become a weapon. At least, the right type of umbrella could. And she prided herself on always having the right type of accessories.

Anna-Marie set a smart pace toward her destination. Cherry Blossom Lane was not nearly as picturesque as its pretty name. Homeless children pickpocketed their way through the street, disappearing into dark alleys when on the brink of being caught. Chimney sweeps called their services. A few pie men ventured this far, offering eel pies for a half penny. It wasn't until she was two blocks away that flower vendors, pot and kettle menders, or milkmaids were found to be peddling their wares and services aloud. Dust collectors hurried from house to house, collecting the ashes swept from the fireplaces. Overall, the bustle and the color on Market Street made poor Cherry Blossom Lane seem like nothing but a dead, barren row of dilapidated buildings.

She had been back to the city only a handful of times over the past years but found nothing much had changed. Even a few faces were the same as ever, though with added lines and wrinkles.

"Hello, pretty lady." The baker held up a basket. "Care for a loaf?"

"Does that line get you a simper and a sale from anyone at all, James?"

"Well, look who it is. Little orphan Anna-Marie. You were just a scrawny thing, last I saw. Trying to filch some bread, if I recall." The baker pulled the basket away. "I assume you can pay this time?"

Anna-Marie gave a curt nod. "Indeed. I'll take three loaves. Have them delivered to Number Thirteen, Cherry Blossom Lane."

"Delivered? To Cherry Blossom Lane?" He shook his head, his double chin wobbling with the motion. "I don't think so."

"You there." Anna-Marie pointed a gloved finger at a girl whose outstretched hand was only inches from relieving the baker of his coin purse. "Cherry Blossom Lane, do you know it."

Frozen, the girl only gulped.

"You can have a bowl of soup, a chunk of bread, and a coin if you deliver these loaves to Number Thirteen." She leaned closer and whispered, "Plus more jobs if you set a smart pace and make it there with all three loaves in hand."

The girl's eyes grew round as saucers.

"Can I trust you to get the job done?"

She nodded. "Yes, miss."

"Good." Anna-Marie settled the bill with James before stepping quickly on.

"You're a fool." The baker called after her. "That chit will sell that bread if she doesn't eat it all herself."

Anna-Marie ignored the man and kept walking. It was a distinct possibility, no doubt about it. But she had seen the awe mixed with the desperation in the little girl's gaze. The child was too curious not to turn up for her bowl of soup and coin. Persuading the child of the real job she had in mind might cost her a bit more than warm food. Or it might not. Hunger was a compelling force, as was loneliness.

She would know.

The two were responsible for the choices she made five years ago…

***

Anna-Marie remembered every vivid detail of the day she was kicked out of Pauper House. At seventeen, you were no longer a young girl who could be leased out for work or for whom there was hope of adoption. At seventeen, you were a burden, a mouth to feed, a responsibility nobody wanted. So, you were sent off with the clothes on your back and an admonishment not to come back, crying for a handout.

Unlike other girls who dreaded the occasion, Anna-Marie had relished the day she gained what she thought was freedom. Spitting at the feet of Godfrey Letchford, she'd turned her back on her past and set out to make her own way. Ay, she knew the limits on women. Still, she had always been smart and a tinkerer to boot. She'd labored under the false impression her skills with mechanical objects would make her a desirable apprentice.

"Good mornin', sir. I've noticed how busy you are." Anna-Marie smiled at the elderly clockmaker. She knew he had no sons, nobody to help with the business. Anna-Marie had done her research the past year, preparing for this day. "I've a steady hand and some experience with repairs of our domestic automaton. With a little learnin', I could be a right help to ya. What do you say?"

"A woman assistant? Are you mad? Escape from one of those asylums, did you? Get out of here before you drive away business with such outrageous talk!"

She'd been desirable, all right, but not for any respectable work. Tradesmen had laughed in her face. Like the clockmaker, shop owners shooed her away, aghast she would even suggest working for them in any capacity other than to tend and sweep, or perhaps make tea. And those were the people who'd been kind.

The less than kind had offered her a position as mistress.

The truly evil had simply pushed her into an alley and tried to rob or take advantage of her.

One such memory made her shudder. It was her third day of so-called freedom. Hungry. Dirty. Cold.

Anna-Marie, out of both coins and options, had trudged dejectedly toward Seven Dials, the warren of the poorest immigrants. The closer she came to the mouth of the square where seven roads poured out, the narrower the space she had to walk. Tenements loomed overhead but all of their inhabitants seemed to have spilled onto the street. A goat bleated as it ran across her path. The number of heads that turned and eyes that flashed in its direction made her certain the poor creature probably wouldn't make it home to its master unless caught quite soon.

And the stench. The smell was almost enough to change her mind. It had definitely decreased her appetite. Fermentation and sewage, manure and death. There were so many vile smiles mingling into one that she was unable to identify the worst. A street brawl broke out to her left. Three women cackled as they entered a gin shop to her right. Everything around her made Cherry Blossom Lane seem to be a shiny haven of cleanliness in comparison. Anna-Marie shuddered.

Still, she walked on. Every avenue she had tried had been a dead end. This was the only course of action she could think of to try next. She'd heard rumors of a workhouse in the Dials that could always find work for the desperate. And she was desperate.

It was another day thick with fog and misery. Pure exhaustion caused her head to drop, her limbs to slow. She stopped watching her surroundings, focusing only on putting one foot in front of the other.

"Well, lookie here. Are you lost, little dollymop?"

Anna-Marie's head jerked up at the vulgar language. "Get lost." She tried to look fierce. Her eyes strayed between the dark gleam in the man's eyes and the empty jug in his hand. From the faint sloshing sound it made, she surmised the man had drunk most of the spirits already.

Taking a couple of steps toward her, he swayed and lurched the last two feet. He grabbed her by the arm and twisted.

"Get off me!" She tried to shake free from the man.

He laughed and twisted harder, forcing her into the alley. Ceramic shattered as he dropped his jug and slapped the other hand over her mouth. One shard cut her leg, but she barely noticed as she squirmed and jerked.

"Now, now." The man shoved her against a crate, bending her over. Holding her in place with his knee, he dropped her arm to lift her skirts.

Terrified, Anna-Marie bit down as hard as she could. She gagged as blood filled her mouth, but it was worth it when the man pulled his hand away with a curse.

The next moments passed in a blur. She screamed out, but she wasn't a fool. Nobody would help an orphan like her. She tried to run. Pain blossomed in her cheek as the man knocked her upside the head. He grabbed her dark hair, jerking her head to the side, and bit down on her neck.

Anna-Marie felt bile in her throat at the thought of what was coming next.

And then, the pressure released.

The man stumbled and fell.

Anna-Marie turned, clutching at her neck. She looked down at her attacker in stunned silence. Blood pooled beneath him.

One second, he was inescapable; the next, he was a lump in the alley.

Slowly, as each heartbeat began to mellow into a normal rhythm, sounds returned and her vision expanded beyond the dead man. Her gaze first met a pair of black boots with deadly spikes embedded in the sides, and all she could think was how badly she wanted a pair of those boots.

Next, she looked above the weaponized boots and black pants, to the scar-covered torso of a man, lean but hard, up past a chiseled chin and crooked nose, into a pair of surprisingly light-green eyes. *The eyes don't match the man*, she thought, studying him slowly as if her brain were working in quicksand. They were bright, cheery even; the man was dark and dangerous.

He allowed her to stare for a full minute before wiping the blade of a short, black knife on a scrap of cloth. Then, he tossed the cloth onto the dead man before sheathing his weapon in leather at his waist.

Realizing for the first time she might still be in danger, Anna-Marie gasped. She backed away, only to find herself up against the same crates she'd just escaped from.

"Please, I don't have any money." Anna-Marie's eyes darted from one end of the alley to the other. Her limbs still felt so weak from fear, she doubted she would make it to either side, but she might as well know which way was closer.

The scarred man reached behind him and tugged a shirt off a barrel, never breaking eye contact as he shrugged into it.

Anna-Marie gulped.

"I'm not here for money."

"Then why? Why did you save me?"

"Because it was in my best interest, of course." The man bowed mockingly in front of her. "Cyrus Blaylock. Procurer. Now…" He straightened. "Off we go."

***

Anna-Marie shook off the memories. It seemed a lifetime ago, yet every detail was clear and sharp in her mind, like it had only just happened. Her body zipped with energy as she turned down a small side street and then left into an even grungier alleyway. Whether that energy was nerves or eagerness, she couldn't tell. She dreadfully feared it was the latter as she searched out the dark figure once more.

A shadow detached from the wall. Short as she was, the figure blocking her path was easily as wide as the rear end of an elephant. In place of flesh and bone, the man had hands made of iron. Half of his face was covered by a metal plate. A mechanical eye focused on her, the unnaturally large pupil somehow growing even bigger.

Anna-Marie stood still, taking stock. Other than the hands and face, she couldn't see any other traces of automaton. She surmised he was simply a modified human. And humans all had their weak points.

For example, the narrowing of his unmodified eye and leer of his mouth as he stepped closer showed that this man had a desire for pretty women unhindered by respect or self-control. As the chubby man lumbered forward, he whistled and wriggled his bushy caterpillar eyebrows at her.

She didn't have time for this.

Snakelike, she tensed, waiting until he was almost close enough to reach for her with one meaty paw then struck out, thrusting the tip of her umbrella into the mechanical eye. A hearty crunch of metal and sickening slurp of flesh sounded as she shoved the eye deep into the socket.

The man reacted predictably, both arms flying to his face to bat the object away. Anna-Marie lunged again—this time, the tip of her umbrella striking soft, vulnerable flesh between the legs.

As she watched the hired muscle drop to the ground with a thud, she grinned. Men always did underestimate the value of the perfect accessory. The hulking form groaned as she stepped on and over him to let herself in the now guard-free door.

She waited a moment as her eyes adjusted. A short, jiggly fellow began to stand up, a deck of cards sprawled on the table in front of him. Anna-Marie held up her hand, palm out. "Don't trouble yourself. Your boss will want to see me. Besides, your buddy in the alley could probably use your help."

Anna-Marie kept walking through the room, grimacing at the black and gray striped wallpaper, far too gothic for her tastes. The rug in the center of the room was red, not rich in tone but darker and reminiscent of dried blood. She wondered if that was on purpose given the nature of the establishment; it would certainly save on the necessity of cleaning. Other than the card tables, very little furniture stood out as the room was only dimly lit by lanterns. She stopped to inspect one at the bottom of the stairs. The lanterns were of the new electric style currently all the buzz.

Hmm. The Procurer must be doing well for himself.

Tucking that thought away for later, she squared her shoulders and ascended the stairs. Her footsteps didn't make a sound on the carpeted treads, but she had no doubt her presence was known.

At the landing, she paused to listen. A scrape of a chair. The thump of a glass. She followed the sounds to her left and pushed open the closest door.

Cyrus Blaylock raised his glass in salute. "Well, well. Aren't you a sight for sore eyes." He let out a low whistle. "Nice boots," he said with a nod to the spikes. His own spiked boots, a newer-looking pair than the ones he wore during their first meeting all those years ago, were propped on the desk as he reclined in his chair.

"I'm not sure your door man would agree, though he undoubtedly will be sore." Anna-Marie watched those laughing green eyes. They were less merry today than she recalled.

Though he acted relaxed, Cyrus was on edge, poised to spring like a panther from his perch at any time. He waved her to a cracked leather chair in front of his desk, then wagged a finger as one would at a naughty child. "Why did you have to go and bust up my best security guard, Anna-Marie? That's not very friendly."

"This isn't a friendly visit."

"Oh. Business, is it?"

She nodded curtly.

"That changes things, then. For a friendly visit, I could forgive your...impatience to see me again. But for business, I'm going to have to charge you for that little camera you broke, my sweet. Tell me, how do you plan to pay?" Cyrus drew out the last word. He dropped his feet to the floor and leaned forward, eyeing Anna-Marie appreciatively. The open collar of his black shirt dipped, revealing a twisted red scar snaking along his chest.

A delicate shiver rippled up her spine. She tried to hide her physical response but saw the darkening of Cyrus's gaze the moment he noticed. The man might be at least eight or ten years her senior, but he hadn't aged a day since she met him. His body was hard lines and muscles. The same danger he lived for made him attractive in an untouchable way.

"With cash," she said quickly.

The devilish man smirked. "A pity. Cash is my least favorite thing."

"Oh? From the looks of things, I'd say you've enjoyed quite a bit of cash since we met. Your little hovel is now classier than…well, classier than you, certainly." The velvet black curtains and black bear rug were pristine. Quite the contrast to the rundown neighborhood in which Cyrus conducted business.

"Cheeky now, are we? I do enjoy cash. I just happen to enjoy it less than other forms of payment." Cyrus grabbed a bottle of whiskey and poured another glass. "Drink?"

"I prefer tea."

"There's no accounting for taste." He wrinkled his nose. "I fear I have no tea kettle."

"That's quite all right. I never travel without one." From a deep fold of her skirt, Anna-Marie produced a metal object. With the press of a button, the object unfolded and twisted until it became a miniature teapot. From one sleeve, she selected a small satchel of tea leaves. From the lace in her hat, Anna-Marie extracted a small silver tea spoon and placed it beside an empty whiskey glass. "I assume you have water," she said dryly.

Once hot water had been poured and the tea leaves were steeping, Anna-Marie flipped open the pocket watch dangling from her corset pocket. Bronze intertwined with silver in an intricate pattern, creating an owl, the wings of which hid the timepiece.

"Shall we discuss business, now? I do have other matters to attend."

"By all means." Cyrus bowed. His green eyes were full of mirth again. "What is it you need me to procure?"

"For now, information." She snapped the watch closed. "After I've learned what I've returned to this dreadful city to learn, I'll also be in need of an airship with a discreet pilot. Can you handle that?"

"Don't you know by now, Miss Pauper? I can handle anything."

The comment took her back again, to the naïve girl she had been. After saving her from the drunk in the alleyway, Cyrus had efficiently whisked her out of the city and into a new life. His confidence and cockiness had quieted even her own fears about the sudden change to her circumstances—no small feat.

Anna-Marie collected her thoughts, choosing to overlook the comment and get down to the matter at hand. She poured tea into the whiskey glass, added a lump of sugar from yet another mysterious pocket, and said, "The information that I'm looking for is twofold. First and foremost, do you know anything about"—*or have anything to do with* she silently wondered—"the disappearances of young girls from the city? They are no longer even in the orphanages."

Cyrus steepled his fingers together. "And the second thing you be wanting to know?"

"The itinerary of Lucifer Banks."

"That second one is so easy, I'll throw it in for free."

Anna-Marie frowned. Cyrus didn't give anything for free. His teasing tone told her she wouldn't like what she was about to hear.

"I'll bite…"

"Please, do," Cyrus interrupted, waggling his dark eyebrows.

With a long-suffering sigh, Anna-Marie ignored the rascally comment. "Lucifer Banks's itinerary... I'm listening?"

"He goes to the same place every day. Every night, as well."

Anna-Marie bit down on her tongue. If she showed Cyrus her impatience, he would only toy with her longer. For such a hardened criminal, the man found extreme humor in the smallest things. It was, unfortunately, one of the things that drew her to him, even when she knew she should be repulsed or frightened, as any wise person would be.

"You're no fun today." He tossed back the last of the whiskey. "Two-oh-seven, Chapel Way."

"The church?"

"The cemetery."

"He's dead?" Disappointment flared. She had been hoping to track down the owner of the orphanage and remind him of his obligations to the girls there. Somewhere public, a ball or soiree with his cohorts, had been her plan. Somewhere he would only be able to agree to larger financial stipends in order to save his philanthropical persona. Now, it seemed that plan was out of steam before she'd even fired it up, figuratively speaking.

"As a doornail." Cyrus pulled a knife from his boot and began cleaning beneath his fingernails.

"Drat it all." Anna-Marie stomped one booted foot.

Cyrus switched to cleaning the nails on his other hand, studying her. "An airship captain, you said?"

"That's right." Anna-Marie frowned at the abrupt change of topic.

"Let me ask you this. Would you be willing to fly with a less experienced pilot if I told you it might help you with your goal to speak with Mr. Banks?"

"But you just said he was dead."

"Ah. His heir, however, is not."

"And you know where he is?"

"For an extra fee, I can schedule you to be onboard an airship with him for a private voyage. What do you say?"

"I say we have a deal."

Cyrus sheathed his knife. Coming around the desk. he spit in his palm, holding it out to her.

Anna-Marie stood, spit in her own hand, and shook. "I've never understood this disgusting custom," she admitted.

"We could cut ourselves and seal the bond with blood, if you like. I'm always a fan of the old ways." He held up his hand to reveal rows of scars.

"No, thank you."

"As I thought. There's something to be said for sealing with a kiss, as well. The bodily fluids still mix up nicely when done right." Cyrus stepped even closer.

Heat radiated from the man in front of her, tempting Anna-Marie to step into it. She schooled her features. "Alas, we've already shaken. You'll find me when you have the information on the girls?"

Cyrus smirked and stepped away. "I will. And Anna-Marie?"

"Yes."

"Don't maim anyone on your way out."

"I shall do my very best."

Chapter Four

Anna-Marie paid close attention to her surroundings, making a quick stop at the apothecary for oil, then the butcher for sausages, and completed her long walk back to Number Thirteen, Cherry Blossom Lane. Without maiming anyone.

She still wasn't convinced Cyrus wasn't involved in the disappearances of young girls in the city, but she couldn't outright accuse the man without proof. And if he *wasn't* involved, his good humor would transform into the foulest of moods, something she preferred to avoid since she still needed him to help her. That's why she planned to do some more digging on her own about the girls' disappearances. Better not to put all her eggs in one basket.

Upon reaching the door of her destination, she sighed at the ruckus that could be heard from the steps. Forget uncovering a plot to steal children, finding the lost girls, and giving everyone a fresh start. Keeping these four girls from killing each other might be a more difficult task.

"Get that horrid broom out of my face!"

Screeching and the bump of furniture sounded.

She marched inside, not bothering to knock. Vivien's continued yells could be heard echoing throughout the house, but Anna-Marie did not turn in the direction of the noise. Instead, she stopped in front of Constantina.

"Come on, old friend. Let's get you fixed up." Anna-Marie pulled a small lever behind the automaton's head to put the machine to sleep. She placed her hands on either side of the dull metal abdomen and rolled Constantina forward, continuing down the foyer to the rear of the house.

The kitchen was small but clean. It wasn't cold, but it wasn't bustling with warmth and activity either. Banged up pots and pans were piled high, waiting to be washed. The floors had clearly not had a good scrubbing in weeks.

As she'd hoped, the ragged little girl from the street was sitting at the table. Her eyes grew large at the sight of Anna-Marie and the automaton domestic servant. Machines in all shapes and sizes were the rage everywhere right now, but it wasn't surprising an orphaned street girl hadn't seen many up close.

No cook was in sight. Anna-Marie made a note to ask the other girls if the orphanage still retained one.

"I see you've made it." Anna-Marie spoke softly as she joined the girl at the table. "Here, let me cut this for you." She slathered a double portion of bread with the last bit of butter she could find.

The girl licked her chapped, pink lips.

"Did anyone let you in?"

"No. I knocked. Honest, I did. Nobody answered. I feared gettin' the bread stolen, so I let myself in." She shrank back as if awaiting a scolding, or worse.

Anna-Marie nodded reassuringly. She touched the girl's hand and smiled. "It's okay. That was smart. I could use some smart people around here."

Vivien's shrieks sounded even closer. Anna-Marie sighed.

"How would you like to work for me? In exchange, you'll have a roof over your head and food in your belly. Coin once a week to buy something for yourself."

"What do I got to do?" the little girl asked around a mouthful of bread, spewing crumbs. Her stomach rumbled for more ever as she stuffed large bites in her mouth.

Before answering, Anna-Marie pulled a small screwdriver out of her sleeve and faced Constantina. She loosened a screw the size of a pinhead and opened a door to the inner workings, or brain, of the automaton. "Hmm." Wrinkles formed above her brow as she bent to concentrate on the gears inside.

The little girl scooted closer, leaning forward in her chair to watch.

"Hand me that rag, would you?"

The girl complied quickly.

The dirty rag became grimier and blackened in no time as Anna-Marie wiped meticulously at the innards of Constantina. She spoke as she cleaned. "Foremost, I'd like you to listen for some information on the streets. No poking around and getting in danger, you understand? Just keeping your eyes and ears open." Anna-Marie turned to face the little girl again with a frown. "You are one of the few girls I've seen. There are rumors most are being taken off of the streets, but I haven't learned where they are being taken or by who." She reached into another pocket for the lubricant purchased that afternoon. With the stopper, she applied several precise drops, turning the gears by hand to fully coat them. "Do you know what I'm talking about?" she asked after closing the small door on the back of the metal head.

The little girl gulped before nodding slowly.

"I thought so." Conscious of how little oil was in the bottle, she chose only a few external joints to place the precious drops. With any luck, it would be enough to reanimate Constantina and make her movements smooth once again.

Before Anna-Marie could press the little girl for information, a crash sounded from the hall. The sound of yells and cries became too deafening to ignore. She checked her pocket watch with a sigh. "For today, I'd be much obliged if you clean up these dishes and stay out of sight until I've straightened out the older girls. Then, this evening, I'll introduce you and show you to your room." She held out a hand. "Speaking of introductions, I'm Anna-Marie."

"Rosie."

"Would you say we have a deal, Rosie?"

The girl shook her hand warily. Anna-Marie could see she had a long road ahead in teaching the girl to trust, but that was to be expected. For now, it was time to teach some different lessons to the young ladies in her charge. It sounded as though they were trying to bring the orphanage down around their ears.

Stepping into the hallway nearly cost Anna-Marie her head. She ducked, just in time to avoid a broom swinging through the air, slamming into the wall next to her. If there had been any portraits or valuables in the orphanage, they would have been unlikely to survive. However, the hall was bare of adornment. Not a knickknack in sight. Even the threadbare rugs were only present in the parlor and study.

"How dare you run this dirty broom over my gorgeous trunk?" Vivien swung the broom again, chasing after Temperance. "I told you to leave my things alone."

"But Anna-Marie said we were to clean, and you wouldn't clean anything with us."

"Enough!" Anna-Marie let out a sharp, piercing whistle. "Vivien, the broom." She held out a hand.

Vivien sneered, slapping the broomstick into her hand harder than necessary. Anna-Marie didn't even flinch.

"Clearly, we will need a more organized approach." Setting the broom aside, Anna-Marie reached inside of a skirt pocket and produced a charcoal pencil and scrap of paper. "I will assign each of you new cleaning duties."

"I'm not some commoner to be used as a maid." Vivien crossed her arms.

Anna- Marie ignored the sassy girl. "Where are Prudence and Patience? I'm only going to go over this once."

"They're cleaning the parlor," Temperance said.

"To the parlor, then." Anna-Marie marched ahead of the girls, expecting them to follow.

They did.

Still, she didn't for an instant let herself believe Vivien's sudden compliance was a sign of a changed attitude. No, she likely just wanted to be around more people to disagree with. Anna-Marie had forgotten what a chore that girl could be.

Upon entering the parlor, they found Prudence and Patience arguing over the arrangement of the pillows on the couch.

"Line up by the fireplace, please. Come on, snip-snap."

With grumbling from Vivien, wide-eyed looks from the twins, and an excited, upbeat attitude from Temperance, everyone lined up. Anna-Marie looked them over. Slouching, frowning, thumb-twiddling. It was a good thing she was simply trying to muster up a house cleaning and not something more important. Not yet, anyway.

"I will be assigning daily chores."

"Hmph."

Ignoring Vivien, she continued. "Each person will be responsible for their own chores. Everyone will pull their weight."

"Even Vivien?" Temperance asked from the relative safety of the opposite side of the fireplace, out of reach of the mean-tempered girl in question.

"Yes."

"No." Vivien spoke at the same time.

"Cleaning is not a spectator sport, Vivien. You will do your fair share if you expect to continue sharing in the lodging and food." Vivien began to protest, but Anna-Marie merely gave another shrill whistle and kept talking. "That brings us to the first order of business. Is there a cook?"

The girls all shook their heads.

"I've been working in the kitchen," Patience said quietly.

"Gruel is all she can cook," Temperance piped up.

Prudence shuffled her feet. "There's no money for food. We, umm…We tried to steal some from the study, but Godfrey always spent everything before coming back here. There wasn't ever a penny to be found."

"Ah. That is no surprise. The lazy drunkard seemed even worse than I remembered. No matter, he's gone. I will teach each of you to cook a bit at a time. For tonight, I've acquired some bread and sausage."

The eruption of gleeful expressions and noises from the girls was deafening. Even Vivien perked up, clasping her hands together in delight, before she hid her expression behind a mask of indifference.

"Let me remind you. If you do not clean, you do not eat." Anna-Marie met each pair of eyes deliberately. "With that, here are your assignments."

With the girls busy at last and the quarreling at a minimum—she had the foresight to assign Vivien the main rooms downstairs and the other girls the upstairs and attic—Anna-Marie returned to the kitchen, where she was pleasantly surprised by the changes she found. The dishes were neatly stacked on the counter, sparkling clean. The floors were swept clean of dirt and debris, and even the windows were no longer flecked with grime. There was no bright sunshine to stream through the clean panes, only the usual dismal gray skies, yet the effect brightened the room even so.

"Rosie, you are simply a miracle worker!"

The small girl scrunched up her face. "Is that good?"

"Indeed." Anna-Marie knelt down in front of her. "It is a very, very good thing. Let's get the dining hall ready to eat, shall we?"

Rosie's mouth dropped open. "You mean, I get to eat again?"

"You do. And we will dine with the other girls, who will be equally happy to see this fluffy bread. Hmm." Anna-Marie tapped her chin. "We'd best hide one loaf for breakfast, or it will all be gone. Can you keep a secret?"

The girl smiled. "Yes!"

"Okay. We'll stash this loaf here on top of the cupboard." Anna-Marie wrapped the bread in a tea towel and, standing on her tiptoes, tucked the bread out of sight. "There. All done."

Rosie helped carry the dishes and set the table as instructed, while Anna-Marie cooked the sausage in the most rust-free pan she could locate. When Rosie returned, Anna-Marie kept her gaze on the sausage, as if she wasn't truly interested in the answer as she asked, "You knew something about the girls being taken, the ones I mentioned earlier, didn't you?" She watched from the corner of her eye as the girl's fingers knotted in her worn dress.

"Only a little." The girl's lip quivered. "My friend Celia was taken. We were together, but I popped out of sight to use the necessary. When I came back, I saw a black wagon pulling away. There were lots of lumps under a dirty green blanket. One of the lumps moved, and Celia's shoe fell off the wagon." Tears welled in her eyes, but she swiped them angrily away. "I was too scared to follow them."

"Thank goodness you didn't."

"What d'ya mean?"

Anna-Marie removed the sausage from the pan, careful not to waste the precious grease. Mercy only knew what they could flavor with it. Then, she turned to the girl and put her hands on her hips.

"Thank goodness you didn't follow that wagon. Those bad people who took your friend would have taken you too. Instead, you're here with me now, and we are going to find them together, safely. You've already given me our first clue—a black wagon."

"Really?"

"That's right," Anna-Marie assured the girl. "Do you remember anything else about the wagon? The horses pulling it? Driver?"

"Tweren't no horses."

"Oh?" She tried to sound casual but Anna-Marie was on high alert. With no horses, this was not your average, poor potato wagon. Rosie might indeed have a clue she would be able to follow up on. Was it possible a steam vehicle had been in the area and not a soul had remarked upon it?

"It was being pulled by two blokes."

"Pardon?" Rosie's comment shattered Anna-Marie's wandering thoughts and any hope of an easy lead to follow. A steam-powered vehicle, wagon or otherwise, would have been noticed. Even if people had been convinced to turn their heads, there were just as many ways they could be convinced to talk about it. But two men pulling a wagon? It was unlikely they received even a second glance. Still. "What did the men look like?" she asked.

"One was skinny like maybe he'd been hungry a while. The other was just a regular bloke, I guess. Both had on these black caps and they were real dirty." She scuffed her toe on the floor. "That's all I remember because I was mostly watchin' the wagon, hoping Celia would get off."

"That is quite all right. You have been very helpful, Rosie. Now, let's go eat, and we will talk about all of this again tomorrow, after a good night's sleep."

Rosie nodded. She dried the rest of her tears and set her mouth in a determined line.

***

"Get a move on. The sausage is getting cold." Vivien pushed Prudence aside.

Patience stepped out of her way without waiting for a similar shove, giving a small head shake. Temperance clamored into a chair ahead of everyone.

"Girls." Anna-Marie clapped her hands for their attention. She did try to reserve the whistle for very serious circumstances, or when she was quite vexed, after all. "Before we begin eating, I'd like to introduce you to someone. This is Rosie."

Shyly, the small girl stepped from behind Anna-Marie's skirts. Rosie stared at her toes until Anna-Marie cleared her throat. Then, she looked up at the older girls with narrowed eyes.

Temperance, never at a loss for words, waved. "Hi. You an orphan too?"

"Yeah." Rosie said the word with bitterness.

"Cool." Temperance slid out another chair. "Come sit by me."

The tension in the room eased, and everyone claimed a chair. The girls reached for bread and sausage. Vivien poked Prudence in the hand with her fork, earning a reproachful glare.

Anna-Marie sighed. One battle at a time.

Chapter Five

The next morning, Anna-Marie stole softly down the hall to the parlor while the girls slept. From the cushions of the settee, she retrieved the metal hair comb. A bit too large to be fashionable, this was not an ordinary comb. Put together with numerous clockwork gears, the comb had a small, built-in sound recorder hidden in plain sight, masquerading as the round center of a delicate flower. The flower's petals arced together to create a miniature horn for collecting sound. The spinning motion, attributed to the gears making the flower turn, was actually the movement of a stylus cutting a groove into a small disc. The grooves captured the sounds and, in a technology Anna-Marie didn't pretend to understand, could be replicated in wax and played back on a different device that "read" the grooves.

Understanding the how or why it worked aside, she had witnessed the playing of such records before. Anna-Marie had everything she needed upstairs in her carpet bag to allow her to listen to the conversations that had taken place in her absence. If the girls knew more than they were telling about disappearances around the city, she would find out.

Satisfied the comb had gone undetected, she tucked it back into hiding and made her way to the kitchen.

There was a chill in the room, but she was happy to see the dishes had been washed and put away last evening, per her instructions. She busied herself stoking the fire in the range, soon working up a sweat. If they were to remain in the orphanage very long, she would look into the newer cooking boxes that used coal gas rather than the monstrous fire box. As if unhappy with her thoughts, the hot plate atop the fire box grew bright red, burning her fingertips as they brushed across.

At her yelp of dismay, a groggy Rosie poked her head from beneath the table. "You okay?"

"Yes, yes. I'm fine." Anna-Marie blew a soft, cool breath across her finger. "What are you doing down here instead of in bed?"

"Bed?" Looking confused, Rosie rubbed sleep from her eyes and stood up. "I thought I was to sleep in the kitchen, like most underservants."

"I didn't bring you here to be a servant. Yes, I need you to do some work for me, but I brought you here to keep you safe. To give you a home with myself and the other girls."

Rosie ducked her head, but not before Anna-Marie saw the wondrous look in her eyes or the smile tease at her lips. She patted the girl on the head. "Go on with you. May as well wake the others to break their fast now."

Rosie ran from the room.

Anna-Marie sucked on the tip of her throbbing finger, listening to the retreating footsteps. A bump at the door behind her made her spin. She grabbed a long, wooden spoon and brandished it before her.

"Easy." Norbert held up a box of coal. "I'll give you a discount for not whacking me with that thing, if you please."

"Bert." Anna-Marie placed the spoon neatly back by the range. "What are you doing here? Didn't you make your delivery yesterday?"

"I came back to make sure Godfrey hadn't returned to make trouble." His eyes dropped to her red finger, which still hovered near her lips. "What have we got here? Are you hurt, Anna-Marie?"

"A tiny burn. I'm perfectly fine."

"Perfectly stubborn, I'd say." Bert clasped her hand gently in his soot-covered one and tugged her to the sink, where he poured a pitcher of cool water over her finger. "It will hurt a day, maybe two. You're lucky. No blisters."

"As I said, I'm fine." She pulled her hand, but Bert did not let go. Slowly, Anna-Marie lifted her gaze to find him studying her intently.

"You left."

Anna-Marie steeled herself against the twisting sensation those two small words stirred up in her stomach. "I told you I was going to."

"I didn't believe you." Bert took a step closer. He let go of her injured hand, running his up her bare arm.

"Norbert—"

The door banged open. Anna-Marie turned quickly, taking a small step away from Bert in the process. He unloaded coal in the coal box, whistling a merry tune.

Anna-Marie took a deep breath. She had not considered that her return to an orphanage of girls and young women would force her into such continuous contact with men. Specifically, men she had tried not to think of for so many years.

Rosie smiled, unaware of any lingering tension, but behind her, Vivien's eyes narrowed.

Of course, the girl rarely lost her pinched, annoyed expression, Anna-Marie reminded herself. It was an unfortunate side effect of being so unhappy.

"Is everyone up?" Anna-Marie asked.

"That's right. Do you need me to do anything else, Anna-Marie?"

Rosie looked at her with something akin to hero worship, a fact that made Anna-Marie even more uncomfortable. "You take the butter in to the table. Vivien, the tea kettle is ready, if you please."

"Not that it would matter if I didn't, I suppose."

"No. It would not," Anna-Marie said flatly.

With a decidedly unladylike huff, Viven wrapped a cloth around the kettle and carried it to the dining hall. Anna-Marie watched her go, then reached into a pocket on her skirt and pulled out a handful of coins.

"Here you go, Bert. Thank you for the coal. I think one delivery a week should suffice for now. Payment will be on time, unlike what you're accustomed to here at Pauper House for Girls." The name of the orphanage on her tongue made her frown, as always. The place had always felt more like a cage than a house.

Doffing his hat, Bert took the dismissal with a smile and a wink on his way out the door.

Yelling erupted from the dining hall beyond the kitchen door. Anna-Marie sighed.

"What's happened this time?" she asked as she pushed open the door.

"Vivien poured hot tea on Prudence!" Temperance pointed.

"On accident," Vivien said.

"You must admit, you've been having a lot of accidents around Prudence since Anna-Marie returned." Patience spoke quietly, but Anna-Marie was surprised to see the steel in the girl's gaze.

"Is this true?"

"No." Vivien glared.

Patience held up a hand, ticking off her fingers one by one. "Ripped the sheets on her bed, singed her hair with the curling tongs, nearly broke her toe when you stepped on her foot. All accidents, according to you."

"But Vivien never burns hair." Temperance frowned. "She won't even let anyone else touch the curling tongs because she says we don't know how to use them."

At any moment, Anna-Marie expected to see steam from Vivien's ears rivaling any coming out of the tea kettle. "That's enough. I believe I see the picture. Vivien, you may dine alone in the kitchen today. When you are ready to treat the others with the respect and kindness due them, you may return."

Vivien slammed the tea kettle onto the table. "Fine. The range is far better company than any of you." She speared one of the remaining sausages and put it on her plate, then added a large chunk of bread, grabbed her cup, and stomped away from the table.

"And Vivien?"

The young woman turned, her lips in a tight, thin line.

"I would be here with or without the advertisement written by Prudence. It was time for me to return. If you have a problem with that, kindly take it up with me directly."

Anna-Marie matched Vivien's long stare until the girl turned and stalked to the kitchen.

"What are we waiting for?" Anna-Marie raised an eyebrow at the remaining girls. "Eat your breakfast. We have a busy day ahead."

The breakfast dishes were being cleared when Patience paused, nose testing the air. She frowned. "Anna-Marie, what's that smell?"

"Smell?" she sniffed. The first acrid scent of smoke reached her nose at the same instant Vivien burst through the door from the kitchen.

"Fire!" Vivien yelled. She pointed behind her. Sure enough, curls of smoke were spreading above the range.

"For the love of tea and biscuits!" Anna-Marie lifted her skirts and ran toward the growing fire.

Chapter Six

Anna-Marie shook her head.

The fire was out, miraculously.

It had taken more water than she would have imagined, and pumping it as fast as humanly possible to haul inside had taken a toll. Of course, nobody had come to help.

Cherry Blossom Lane wasn't of interest to patrols. Not a single neighbor either noticed or cared. None of the emergency water-hydrant automaton engine responders, known simply as *Waters* and equipped with ten gallons of water in their "torso", that were available at the fire engine establishments in the couture districts of London were anywhere close so she could not even borrow one without asking, had she been so inclined. They were another of Uncle Ernest's many inventions which served the elite only.

Letting out a sigh that was a combination of relief and frustration, Anna-Marie scanned the room again. Vivien said the fire was an accident—a tea towel too close to a hot spot. Anna-Marie had other thoughts on the matter, but she chose to keep them to herself. It wouldn't do any good to cast blame. Once again, due to the destitute condition of the orphan house, no investigation would be forthcoming into the source of the fire.

She wished for a moment's respite but knew such a rest wasn't an option. Rosie's cleaning had been for nothing. The kitchen was now covered in sticky black residue from the smoke. The range was useless, a charred heap of twisted metal. A few cabinets were singed, one completely burnt.

If she and the girls were to eat, she had to do something about the state of the kitchen.

"Vivien, you can see to the regular chores today." Anna-Marie looked about the room. "The rest of you, get to work on the kitchen, if you please. See what you can do to remove the soot, haul bits of the range out back. I'll pop over to the blacksmith and see if he has anything we can use for cooking on in the meantime."

Vivien scowled. Patience nodded. Prudence and Temperance were still looking a bit shell-shocked, staring at the smoldering coal box and blackened cabinets.

"Come, come. Don't just stand there. Things aren't going to clean themselves, you know."

Temperance's mouth popped shut in a comical snap.

Vivien all but snarled as she spun on her heel and flounced from the room. "I'm going to lie down. I could have died in that fire," she called over her shoulder.

"It's really too bad that Constantina is falling apart." Patience frowned. "If she wasn't, maybe it could have all cleaned itself, or at least she could have cleaned it rather than us inhaling this ghastly smoke for hours to do it."

Prudence stared after Vivien. "I guess she won't be eating tonight."

"Will any of us?" Rosie asked quietly.

"Of course, we shall." Anna-Marie consulted the delicate owl-shaped pocket watch dangling from her vest. "Now, I'll be back in a few hours. Patience, that is a marvelous point. Before I go, let me show you a bit about programming Constantina. Perhaps she can pull a bit of Vivien's weight about the place."

Patience obediently followed Anna-Marie from the kitchen to the foyer. "Is it terribly hard?" she asked.

"To give instructions to Constantina?"

"No. To tinker and build automatons, steam or clockwork machines." She twined her fingers around the end of her braid. "You know, like you built Constantina."

Anna-Marie considered the question, turning her full gaze on Patience. "Anything is possible when you put your mind to it. Although"—she frowned—"it is easier when you have someone to teach you."

"Can you teach me?" Patience asked.

"I can. Eventually." Anna-Marie turned to the domestic automaton. "For today, however, watch closely so you can change instruction cards and get Constantina back on track with some housekeeping chores."

As the two worked, Anna-Marie noted the way Patience focused, nodding from time to time, without once interrupting. She wondered if the girl had comprehended the process fully. "Would you like to give it a try?" she asked.

Patience rolled up the sleeves of her dress and leaned forward. She closed her eyes just a few seconds before opening them and swiftly removing the stack of instruction cards, leafing through them until she found what she wanted, and returning the others to a small compartment. With precise movements, she grabbed the second to smallest tool from Anna-Marie's hand and inserted it into the correct hole, turning counterclockwise. A panel opened, and Patience carefully lifted two prongs. Removing the current instruction card, she replaced it gently with the new one.

Anna-Marie nodded in satisfaction as Patience closed and latched the compartment.

"How was that?" Patience asked, eyes sparkling with excitement.

Anna-Marie, hiding her own smile, twisted a knob, and Constantina whirred to life. "Let's find out."

Before she finished her sentence, Constantina glided smoothly away from her docking station. The automaton hummed gently as she whisked to the parlor. There, the machine began to fold blankets and fluff cushions.

Unfortunately, one mechanical arm pinched a pillow too firmly. A hole ripped, and feathers flew about the room as Constantina continued her task of tidying, unaware. While they watched, the torn fabric caught on a stack of paper, knocking them into a tea cup. Overall, the parlor was a larger mess than it had been before. Constantina rolled out of the room and back to her docking station.

"Hmmm." Anna-Marie placed a hand on her hip. "Not what I had in mind. It seems

Constantina may need more than just a dab of oil and a change of cards. Something's faulty."

Patience stood silently by with both hands clasped to her mouth, mortified.

"There, there." Anna-Marie patted her shoulder. "Almost all first attempts go wrong somewhere. Besides, I believe it is Vivien's job to clean the parlor, correct?" She winked.

Patience laughed out loud. "I believe you are right. I'll just go help in the kitchen."

Anna-Marie retrieved her overcoat and umbrella, patting Constantina on the head as she passed through the foyer and out the front door. She hoped she could find the problem with the domestic automaton. Constantina was the one friend she'd had as a girl in the orphan house, her one constant. While other girls came and went, or stayed to play and fight, Constantina could be counted on to be the same every day.

She shook off her thoughts. Now was no time to be maudlin. She had a blacksmith to see and a kitchen to salvage.

Today's gray skies were no different than yesterday, or many previous days for that matter, yet Anna-Marie could feel the rain coming. The air was heavy with it. The smell drifted on the breeze. Setting a brisk pace, she arrived at the smithy in no time.

The clang of metal striking metal rang loudly.

Three men worked around a circular forge. Axles, fire pokers, pots—several finished objects stacked around the open shop, along with heaps of metal that must be in-between stages Anna-Marie couldn't recognize as having a purpose yet.

"Ma'am." A burly man wiped his hands on a long, leather apron. "Are you picking up an order?"

"Not today." Anna-Marie wasn't the least bothered at being mistaken for a servant. It might make her task easier. Servants were known to barter, after all. "I've come to see if you can make an open range. You see, we lost ours in a fire today, and there are many girls to feed."

The smith shook his head. "Not much call for ranges. Gas ovens are all the uppity folk want. I don't make 'em here."

Anna-Marie frowned. "Perhaps you have something else we can use? A castoff? Dented pieces of cookware?"

"I have the shell and rod for a bottle jack, but I don't make the clockwork pieces for turnin' it," he said. "You'll have to get those somewhere else."

Anna-Marie nodded. "How much?" she asked as the blacksmith rolled the metal pieces in paper and tied them with string like a butcher would meat.

He named a price, and after only a moment or two of haggling, Anna-Marie paid what she considered a fair sum. With the parcel in hand, she stepped back into the street and tilted her face to the gray skies. Rain would be most welcome after the oppressive heat of the forge.

Though keen to rush out and find the parts for the bottle jack and start tinkering, Anna-Marie turned not in the direction of the industrial district, but to the marketplace. Conscious of the dwindling supply of coin in her pocket, she haggled for bruised fruits and hard cheeses.

As she stopped at a third stall, she pretended to study the wares while allowing her eyes to scan the streets.

There, behind the flower cart…

A red-headed waif lingered too long to be a pickpocket, yet he wasn't hawking flowers or hailing pedestrians. He was watching her. Anna-Marie had sensed she was being followed since leaving the blacksmith. The boy was good. He had stayed out of sight longer than she predicted. But now, the game was up.

Hefting her parcel closer, just in case, Anna-Marie strolled to the flower cart and bent to sniff one of the blooms. "You have a message for me?" she asked.

The boy nodded. "It's from—"

"Shh. I know who it's from." Anna-Marie stood and smiled at the flower vendor, a young woman with a babe on her hip, who looked at her with suspicion. "What did he say?"

"He said to come for tea."

Anna-Marie raised an eyebrow. It was not the message she expected. "That's all?"

"'Twas all he said." The boy shrugged, then held out a hand.

Anna-Marie sighed before placing a ha'penny in his palm. She didn't begrudge the boy money earned. She did wish he would see the benefit of it and not send it straight to Cyrus's pockets, however.

Tea.

With Cyrus Blaylock.

She sighed again, and this time, the flower vendor scowled until Anna-Marie plucked a blossom from the cart and paid her. Then, the woman was all smiles.

Everything was quiet when Anna-Marie arrived at Number Thirteen.

Too quiet.

She eased inside, carefully placing her parcel in the coat closet and the flower on a wobbly table in the foyer. Constantina remained at her docking station, as she'd left her.

Anna-Marie listened.

There was no bickering or yelling. Not even a scuffle.

She slipped down the hallway. Noticing the parlor door ajar, she peeked inside and had to hide a chuckle.

Patience and Prudence were fast asleep on the settee, leaning against each other as if they'd dozed off mid-conversation. On the floor before the cold hearth, Temperance and Rosie slept on cushions, dust-rags in a high pile beside them.

The room itself sparkled, explaining the exhaustion of the four girls. The old rug had been rolled up into the corner, and even the notched and scuffed hardwood floors had benefited from a good scrubbing.

Anna-Marie inspected the rest of the rooms downstairs. The kitchen…well, the kitchen was as good as could be expected. Each and every living space was fresh and tidy. Even upstairs. It was when she reached the last bedroom and found it empty that she had to admit the more likely reason for the quiet and restfulness of the house.

Vivien was gone.

High to low, the girl was nowhere to be found. Anna-Marie wavered between frustration and worry. It would be just like Vivien to wander off instead of helping with chores. Yet, the missing girls were still a big problem. So far, only younger children had disappeared from the surrounding population, but that didn't mean Vivien hadn't found trouble for herself.

Making no effort to quiet her steps—in fact, Anna-Marie stomped just a bit louder than necessary—she returned to the parlor. As expected, the girls were awake and trying to pretend she hadn't almost caught them sleeping. She wouldn't tell them it was too late and rob them of their excited air of secrecy.

One matter, however, she did not wish to remain secret. "Where is Vivien?"

Temperance opened her mouth to answer, but it turned into a wide yawn.

Patience spoke for the group. "Viven went out only half an hour after you left. She insisted she would be the one to repair the kitchen and wouldn't hear of doing 'servant's work,' as she called the cleaning."

Anna-Marie took out her pocket watch, rubbing her thumb over the wide eyes of the owl, wishing to borrow some wisdom from the creature. "And she didn't say where she was going?"

"Said it was none of our affair." Rosie's mimicry of Vivien's stuffy voice made everyone giggle.

Even Anna-Marie relaxed. Slightly. Vivien had not been gone an hour yet, if the girls were correct about the time. She would hopefully return before Anna-Marie left for tea. If not, then there would be time for worry.

With that thought in mind, she clapped her hands together. The girls came to attention.

"You've done an exemplary job completing your tasks, and Vivien's, today. As you all know, the kitchen needs work before we can safely cook meat again. I did bring some fruit and cheese back for a midday meal." She pointed to the younger two girls. "Temperance and Rosie, please get the food from the foyer and prepare it and the dining table for eating."

After the girls had skipped away, Anna-Marie looked back to the twins. So different in personality and appearance, their sisterly affection for one another was apparent, standing side by side, arm in arm. "I have a meeting and must go out again just before teatime. I'd like for you two to take measurements and make a list of clothing—

necessities only, understand?—that is needed for each of you and the others."

Patience nodded, eager to prove herself.

Prudence flushed as she cleared her throat. "Gowns only? Or underthings as well?"

"Sizes for everything. We may only have enough for one new set of clothing each, but I'd like you all to be more comfortable, and you can't be comfortable when you look and feel shabby, or when your sleeves are two sizes two small."

"But where will we get the money?" Prudence wouldn't meet her eyes as she whispered.

"You leave that to me."

Two heads bobbed.

"That's that, then." Anna-Marie tapped her chin thoughtfully, then noticed the girls still staring at her. "Go on, to lunch with you."

When she had the parlor to herself, Anna-Marie closed the doors and poked around in the settee to retrieve the hidden hair comb. With deft fingers, she removed the delicate disk from the comb's flower and replaced it with a new one before hiding the comb again.

Upstairs, she braced a chair below her doorknob. No lock, but she'd rather the girls think she was odd for barricading the door than them barge in unannounced as she listened to the disc.

With the disc gently between her fingernails, she placed it on the small box and then nudged the tiny needle down to settle into a groove. With the larger horn in place, she wound the crank and waited. Listening was a concentration in frustration, as usual. The sounds were soft, muffled by the cushions, thanks to the need to hide the device, and there were intermittent pauses of silence when nobody was in the room to record.

Anna-Marie heard footsteps, heavy footsteps, coming up the stairs. As she leaned over to lift the needle, the faint humming of the recording turned to soft voices. She put her ear up to the horn to listen.

"What did you take?"

"I don't know what you're talking about."

It was Tempy's voice accusing and Vivien who pretended ignorance. Imagine that. Anna-Marie silently wished the person on the stairs would slow down so she could hear everything.

"From the desk. I saw you take paper out of the drawer when Anna-Marie left this morning."

"You're wrong. And even if you weren't, I suggest you keep your nose to yourself before someone cuts it off."

The argument ceased.

It was just as well, for seconds later, squabbling erupted. It was at the landing, from the sounds of it.

Anna-Marie hid the disk in one of many pockets and put the miniaturized gramophone in a pile of dirty clothes.

"What's going on now?" she asked, stepping out of her room.

"Vivien is back, but she won't say where she's been."

Vivien crossed her arms, ignoring Temperance, who—from what Anna-Marie could tell—was the only one of the girls who didn't fear the older girl's foul temper.

"The girls said you were finding a solution for the cooking problem. Were you successful?" Anna-Marie kept her tone nonchalant. Antagonizing Vivien further surely wouldn't get anywhere. She wished the younger girls would learn that as well. Honey and flies, and all that. Oh well, another lesson for another day.

"I was." Like a peacock, Vivien preened and puffed herself up. "Norbert is going to come have a look this evening. He even promised to bring fish when I told him we had nothing to eat."

Anna-Marie closed her eyes and breathed deeply. She had enough on her plate without Vivien's dramatics, she reminded herself. "Splendid," she said, a half-smile firmly in place. "If you'll excuse me, I must be going."

"Again?" Vivien scoffed. "How typical. You said you were coming back to help, but all I ever see you do is leave." She turned on her heel and slammed the door to her bedroom.

Temperance glared at the closed door. "At least, with so few girls, nobody has to share a room with her royal pain in the rear."

Anna-Marie had to agree. "Quite the bright side, if perhaps the only one."

Chapter Seven

"How is your tea?"

Anna-Marie's brows drew together before she answered. "Surprisingly palatable. One might even say, good."

Cyrus's mouth twitched in amusement. "Careful with the heavy compliments. They might go to a man's head."

"Your new and improved tea services aside, why did you ask for this meeting today?" Anna-Marie placed her black and gold teacup down on the matching saucer.

Black and gold. Seriously, who used black crockery? Cyrus must have custom-ordered it. The man was a puzzle. Unfortunately for him, Anna-Marie only liked puzzles when she had all of the pieces, and with Cyrus, some pieces were definitely hidden.

"I have a lead."

"On the girls?"

Cyrus cocked his head. "Somewhat. More of a lead on a person interested in acquiring more girls."

Anna-Marie didn't like the sound of that. "Meaning?"

Cyrus leaned forward. "An associate agreed to deliver girls two nights from now. We can have someone follow them, find out where he keeps them or if there are any of the other missing girls still in the city."

"We?" Anna-Marie asked sharply. "What's in it for you?"

"Let's just say, I don't like the rumors I've heard. This guy, he's trying to cut in on my territory. Calls himself 'Jack of all Traders,' and I think that Jack and I are due a little chat." His expression darkened.

Anna-Marie shivered before Cyrus wiped the sinister scowl from his face.

"I do need something from you." He smiled.

Raising an eyebrow, she waited.

"Girls."

"Excuse me?" Anna-Marie stood, knocking her chair over.

"For the meeting to take place, my associate has to show up with girls for sale or trade. No girls, no chance to find out where this Jack is hiding out." Cyrus splayed his palms. "That's all I've got for you."

It was Anna-Marie's turn to scowl. She fixed Cyrus with a gaze so fierce a lesser man would have backed down. Of course, Cyrus only smiled wider, the horrid man. Anna-Marie paced.

And paced.

"I'll go," she said, turning back to Cyrus. "Your associate can give me over to the Jack fellow. If you can follow, fine. If not, I'll sort it myself when he takes me to the other girls."

Cyrus slowly shook his head. "While I support your decision to sell yourself in whatever way you wish"—Cyrus waggled his eyebrows—"the demand for girls is specific. Under fourteen."

Anna-Marie stomped one booted foot. "For the love of tea and biscuits."

"So, I ask again. Do you have girls to use as bait?"

Anna-Marie closed her eyes. She prided herself on being practical, not emotional. It was time to remember that. "I believe so. Send someone around tonight for my answer. If we do this, no mistakes. We make it look like a legitimate abduction so the girls are under no suspicion. I don't want them to be in more danger than necessary. And I'm coming with you when we follow them." She turned on her heel without waiting for an answer, sweeping from the room in a whirl of skirts.

Anna-Marie walked until she felt she was reasonably in control of her emotions again. She entered Number Thirteen and was surprised by the sound of laughter. Hanging her coat and umbrella up, she followed the sound to the dining hall.

Bert stood, the center of attention, playing an accordion and singing silly poems as each girl laughed or clapped loudly. Unnoticed, Anna-Marie watched from the doorway. Even Vivien looked downright pretty as she smiled and fluttered her lashes when Bert's attention moved to her.

"A voice as sweet as a morning bird song, hair so fair and long, a vision lovely to any poor chap, but oh beware if her temper does snap." His accordion playing picked up speed. "Watch out, fellas, for this one, the loud and proud Vivien."

Anna-Marie rolled her eyes, shocked Vivien hadn't taken offense to any part of Bert's nonsense. She allowed the frivolity to continue with Rosie's turn next, but soon, Bert glanced her way, and his songs ceased.

"Why, Anna-Marie! Do you fancy a turn?"

"No, I do not. Thank you, Bert." She pointed at the empty plates around the table. "I don't suppose there's any left for me?"

"Of course, there is!" Temperance ran to the kitchen and returned with a plate of cold smoked fish.

"We wanted to wait for you," Rosie said softly. "But Vivien told us you might not come back."

Vivien stiffened, but Anna-Marie ignored the cantankerous girl. Instead, she placed a hand on Rosie's shoulder. "I will always come back. Don't you worry."

"I brought you a few other things." Bert pushed open the kitchen door.

Anna-Marie followed, wrinkling her nose as the lingering smell of smoke assaulted her senses. Maybe she could go out and look for flowers in the garden to freshen things up tomorrow.

"Thank you." She accepted a newspaper-wrapped bundle from Bert. The smoked meats would last a few days and could be eaten cold if need be.

"Are you going to need a new coal box?"

"I suppose. Though if you find something from scrap that will do…We don't need anything new or large," Anna-Marie answered.

"What's this?" Bert nudged the parcel in the corner with his boot.

Anna-Marie finished eating and then scooted around him to unwrap the clockwork bottle jack. "This is my solution to roasting meat without the full range. It is missing a few cogs but once I have those, it should do nicely."

"I'll get them."

"You don't have to do that."

Bert laid a hand on Anna-Marie's arm. "I pass a factory that makes them every day. No trouble."

"Fine." Anna-Marie dipped two fingers into the pouch hanging at her waist. She deposited several shillings into the pocket on Bert's coat, knowing he wouldn't accept it otherwise. "Hopefully that will be enough."

Once Bert was gone, Anna-Marie sent Prudence and Patience to gather the measurements she'd asked them to acquire. Vivien had disappeared up the stairs the moment Bert and Anna-Marie had gone into the kitchen. That left Rosie and Temperance to clear the table and wash up the dining hall, as she'd hoped.

"Girls, can I speak to you for a moment?"

Two young heads nodded enthusiastically.

"You both have heard me say I want to get to the bottom of the girls going missing, yes?" She steepled her hands together, fingers tapping as she forged ahead. "There might be a way, but it is dangerous, and I don't particularly like it. However, there might not be another chance."

"Another chance for what?" Temperance asked.

"Another chance to follow someone to the exact location that the girls are being taken."

Rosie crossed her small arms. "But you said followin' them was a bad idea."

Anna-Marie nodded. "It is a horrid idea if one is alone. For the opportunity that I'm talking about, I would have some very capable help to do the following."

"Then what are you waiting for?" Rosie narrowed her eyes. "Celia and the other girls, who knows what's happenin' to any of them."

Exhaling slowly, Anna-Marie explained. "I'm happy to do the following. The problem arises from the bait."

"Bait?" Temperance frowned.

"That's right. If we are going to have a trail to follow, first that means letting young girls get taken."

"She means us," Rosie said.

Temperance looked between Rosie and Anna-Marie. "And if we get taken, you'll follow us and get us out."

"I understand if you don't want to do it." Anna-Marie watched the girls closely. "We can call it off, forget all about it. I'm sure eventually I could find another way."

"I'll go." Rosie's lip trembled, but she nodded. "I'll go. I want to save Celia."

Temperance bit her lip, and then she, too, nodded. "I always hate to be alone if something is scary. I'll go with Rosie." She leaned over and hugged the younger girl. "At least we will be together, and we can help each other."

Chapter Eight

The next evening, Bert delivered the cogs as promised. He brought a three-sided coal box as well.

"Oh, Bert! Whatever would we do without you?" Vivien gushed.

Behind Vivien's back, Prudence rolled her eyes and mimicked the fawning girl.

Anna-Marie, lost in thought over the latest note from Cyrus, ignored them all. She made quick work of setting the clogs in place, much to the disappointment of Patience, who'd been hoping to help or learn.

Bert, with his tall lanky frame and long arms, hung the bottle-jack easily from a beam in the kitchen so it swung above an open spot where a fire could be built.

"Anna-Marie, is it okay if I have another go at programming Constantina?" Patience asked after Bert left.

"Hmm. Sure, if you'd like," Anna-Marie answered, without looking up from the scrap of paper.

"What are you reading?" Vivien crossed her arms.

"A list." Anna-Marie inspected the bottle-jack, nodded, and strolled to the parlor. "Temperance, Rosie. Would you care to accompany to pick up some meat?"

"Tonight?" Rosie tilted her head. "I thought we were going tomorrow."

"Going where?" Vivien huffed. "Really, Anna-Marie. I wasn't finished speaking with you. What do you have a list of? And what are we supposed to eat? Bert didn't bring any more fish, and we're out of that bruised fruit."

"Because someone ate half of it in one sitting," Prudence murmured, earning a cold stare.

"That's precisely where we're going. To get food now that we can cook. We shall be back in no time." With the paper safely tucked in a pocket, Anna-Marie raised her eyebrows at the younger girls playing a game of jacks by the hearth. "Spit, spot," she snapped her fingers. "Let's go, girls."

"Anna-Marie," Rosie spoke as they walked down the steps to the cobblestone street below.

"Hold that thought a moment." Anna-Marie shushed her with a finger. Only when they'd traipsed two blocks down and were out of sight of the orphanage did she turn to Rosie and allow her to continue.

"I thought the plan was to go out tomorrow." She scrunched her nose. "And are we not telling the older girls?"

Anna-Marie answered in a whisper. "The plan is to take the meeting tomorrow and follow you to Celia and the others. However, the less people who know the plan, the safer you and Temperance remain. Understood?"

When both girls nodded, Anna-Marie motioned for them to keep walking and continued.

"For today, we need you to be seen. We need the person who is looking for girls to know you are in the neighborhood so he won't suspect a trap." Anna-Marie stopped at a cart of nuts and selected a small bag of chestnuts and another of hazelnuts. She tied them together and looped the string around her wrist. "So, we will do what I told Vivien and the others—we will shop for meat and food. And we will take our time."

Temperance and Rosie soon forgot anything but the excitement of shopping and tasting. In her life on the streets, Rosie had stayed on the run more often than anything. Temperance had spent her time at the orphanage in the shadow of the older girls, barely allowed to tag along and, especially in recent times, not leaving the walls of the orphanage often.

The busy market street was crowded. The sun had deigned to show itself today, biting through the typical gray skies to shed a little warmth and extra joy. Couples strolled hand in hand. Business men stepped briskly on their way. Shopkeepers and vendors of all types called greetings and tried to attract each passerby.

"Oh, Rosie, isn't this divine?" Tempy sighed in delight as Anna-Marie gave them money to buy their own apples.

Anna-Marie smiled at the carefree girls, even as her gut tightened to consider the danger she would be putting them in tomorrow. She shooed them away to eat their prizes on a nearby stoop as she selected meat from the butcher, haggling for the best cuts and lowest prices.

"You're a thief, a thief, you know," the butcher said at last. "I'm practically giving away this meat."

Anna-Marie placed the agreed-upon sum in his hand and held her hands out for the parcel. "But you can take comfort in knowing you're helping to feed those two hungry young girls over there." Anna-Marie dipped her head to the side.

"What girls?" the man scowled.

Anna-Marie jerked around in time to see an apple come rolling from the mouth of an alley. She dropped the meat, thanked her good sense for split skirts with pants beneath, and bolted down the alley. Anna-Marie hoped desperately to see the girls goofing off, but the sick feeling roiling through her belly sensed it wasn't to be.

Two men, one burly and one tall and thin, were carrying the girls draped over their shoulders. Unmoving, the girls looked like mere rag dolls. Anna-Marie ran faster, her red boots gobbling at the distance.

Catching sight of her, the men sped up. Soon, she was no longer gaining but losing the men and the girls. From alley to alley, she ran. Her lungs ached.

"Oi, lad!" She grabbed a boy from beside a dumpster, hauling him to his feet in one motion. "You know The Procurer?"

Wide-eyed, he nodded.

"You tell him to get to this alley and be quick about it. Tell him Anna-Marie said tomorrow's business just came *unbuttoned*," she raised her eyes and said the word slowly and clearly. "Tell him I said he better come button it back up again. Immediately!" Not waiting for a reply, she continued her chase. After a dozen or so feet, she ripped a button from her coat and dropped it, doing the same after similar intervals. She had to be careful, though her coat had more buttons than most she would run out at some point. She could have used the hazelnuts but they would have been found and eaten by any child or beggar on the corner.

Now, she could only hope Cyrus would pick up on her message, and her trail.

Chapter Nine

Anna-Marie huddled behind a stack of crates.

The unexpected chase had been long. Eventually, she'd hidden and pretended to lose the men, stopping in an alley and calling out as if she'd lost sight of the girls. As she hoped, the men slowed their own progress and resumed their arrogant walk with their captives in tow.

Though she might have been able to catch the men off guard and subdue them, it was not the time to show off. Anna-Marie knew the odds of taking on both men, as well as keeping the two girls safe and getting them away, were slim. She also knew, if by some miracle she accomplished all of that, their opportunity to find out where girls were being taken would be gone. The men would be spooked and unlikely to risk being caught again.

So, Anna-Marie did the only thing she could do. She crept slowly and quietly after them, ducking in doorways and crouching in filthy piles of garbage to avoid detection any time the men checked their surroundings—which, thankfully for her, wasn't too often. And she had dropped button after button. Fingering the dangling threads on her coat, she scowled. Cyrus better find her or he would owe her a replacement coat for his incompetence.

Anna-Marie risked another look around the crates. In this area, the lack of street lights or homes with glows thrown from the windows was a boon for staying hidden. On the opposite side of the coin, it made seeing what was happening all the more difficult.

The men were bringing the girls out of the warehouse. The children were awake and squirming now, but muffled cries and grunts made her assume gags had been inserted in their mouths to maintain silence.

The beefy man turned, and Anna-Marie ducked back, hoping she hadn't been spotted. The fact they were once again moving the girls had her worried. They were already in the crummiest area, the smallest docks and warehouses on the east end of the Thames. If this wasn't the final destination, she shuddered to think what was. And where in the world was Cyrus? Was he coming?

A very real splash interrupted Anna-Marie's silent worries. She popped up for another look, and her heart dropped into her stomach. The men had placed the girls in the bottom of a skiff and shoved off from the dock.

Anna-Marie frantically eyed the shoreline. There was only one other boat. It was upside down on the dock, wide enough to need at least two people to row it. She squinted, hoping to see a steam motor or other contraption that would make it possible to man the boat herself. Seeing nothing, she clenched her fists in frustration.

"Oh, hang it all!" Anna-Marie had just sprung up from hiding to take a chance on the bigger boat, regardless of the difficulties, when an arm wrapped roughly around her midsection and a hand captured her mouth. She was pulled back down, out of view.

"What was that?" one of the men asked.

The other grunted. "Quit trying to get out of the work and come help."

Quietly, the owner of the arms holding her whispered, "Shhh. Don't even think about using those boots on me. They were my own design, and it wouldn't be right."

Anna-Marie grew still, though she definitely did not relax. Cyrus removed the hand from her mouth but not her waist.

"Unhand me," she whispered through clenched teeth. "They're going to get away."

"That was the point, remember?" His breath tickled her ear.

"But we can't follow them on the river!" she insisted. "We weren't prepared. They took the girls too early."

"Wait."

Before Anna-Marie could ask what in blazes they were waiting for, she heard footsteps. The footsteps were running.

"Oi, ya blighters. Wait for me!" The running man was coming straight toward them, hollering the whole way.

Anna-Marie stiffened, but he never broke stride. Instead, with a sly wink at Cyrus, he went right past as if they weren't there at all.

She stared, mouth agape, as the man flagged down the skiff. He held up a girl. Even in the dusky light, it was apparent the little girl was dressed in fine clothes—much too fine to be someone off the streets.

The man waved. "I've got a package for Jack of all Traders. Word is, this here was the way to bring her."

Cyrus loosened his grasp, but Anna-Marie barely noticed, so intrigued was she by the scene unfolding. The man wore rags befitting a call-on man of the docks but carried himself in a way belying his appearance. At least to Anna-Marie.

The men on the boat mustn't have noticed anything odd, or they plain didn't care. After a shared look, they allowed the boat to drift to the other side of the dock and rowed it close enough for the man to step in. He settled the young girl much more gently than Temperance and Rosie had been treated.

"Where's the gag?" the big fellow asked.

"She's a mute," the newcomer answered. "Are we going, or we stayin' here to blather on all night?"

A splash of oars sounded. Anna-Marie waited a moment and then peered around the crates. The glow of a cigarette followed by another shown in the darkness as the boat rounded a bend.

"Well, that's just lovely now, isn't it? You…You…Argh!." Anna-Marie stood and waved her hands in frustration. "Come on, then. Don't just stand there."

"Where are we going?" Cyrus trailed nonchalantly behind as Anna-Marie marched to the bank of the river. "Why, Anna-Marie, you surprise me. Planning on a midnight swim, are we?"

"No, I am not planning on swimming. I am planning on you getting in this boat and helping me follow those kidnappers." Anna-Marie shoved the boat, budging it an inch. She glared back at Cyrus. "Quit hulking over there uselessly and help me get this thing in the water."

"Have you ever been on a boat?"

"I don't see how that is relevant," Anna-Marie huffed, giving the boat another push.

Cyrus chuckled, a low, throaty sound.

Anna-Marie shivered from a non-existent breeze.

"I assure you that it is relevant. I would prefer to have an experienced hand if I'm going to steal a boat, not someone who doesn't know the fore from the aft or the seat from the paddle." Cyrus placed a hand on her shoulder. "You see, I'm not in the mood for a dunk in the Thames. That water could kill a person, you know."

Anna-Marie shrugged away from Cyrus. What she wouldn't give for her umbrella right now. Of all the evenings to leave it at home, this was a terrible one. "What do you propose we do?"

"We wait."

"Wait. Wait." Anna-Marie fisted her hands on her hips. It was either that or ring the infuriating man's neck, which seemed at cross-purposes with gaining his assistance in the boat matter. "You keep saying *wait*. This was your scheme that has gone awry, may I remind you. Now, the girls are gone, on the way to who knows what fate, and instead of following, as per the plan, you want to wait."

"Yes." Cyrus, perhaps seeing the unflappable Anna-Marie was moments away from throttling him, explained. "Everything is going according to plan. The men who took the girls tonight are working for me. Your reaction, and that of the girls, needed to show genuine fear for the ruse to work."

Anna-Marie narrowed her eyes. "You lied."

"I lied." He nodded.

"And the third man?" Anna-Marie asked, recalling the wink.

Cyrus nodded again. "Also working for me. In case the first two have thoughts of double-crossing. The third man…Well, he has a debt that will be cleared after this. He is to report the location to me before breakfast. And the little girl, that's his niece. I find motivation to be an important factor in business dealings."

"Even shady ones, apparently," Anna-Marie muttered.

In the moonlight, she could see the hard glint in Cyrus's eyes as he leaned toward her. "Especially shady ones."

"Fine." She pulled out her watch, taking comfort in the familiar cool metal, the texture of the design beneath her fingertips. The time was difficult to make out until the moon peeked from behind the fog and clouds. "It's time I head back to the orphan house. I'm sure the girls are worried. I shall be at your office before breakfast. Tomorrow, we *will* get the girls back and find out what is going on once and for all."

Cyrus tipped his head in acknowledgment and, with one last grin, disappeared down an alley.

A gentleman would have insisted upon seeing a lady home safely. Anna-Marie rolled her eyes at herself. Cyrus was no gentleman, and she was no lady, only an orphaned girl grown into a determined woman. She was able to take care of herself.

A small piece of her pride insisted Cyrus knew that too.

Chapter Ten

Anna-Marie tiptoed into the hall.

It was the wee hours of the morning. She had hoped the girls would be asleep but couldn't believe her luck they actually were. As she walked to the stairs, a soft noise from the parlor made her pause. She entered that room to find Patience and Prudence asleep on the sofa again. It looked like they had tried waiting up for her after all. Anna-Marie quietly added a log to the dwindling fire before going upstairs.

In her room, Anna-Marie removed her hat and pins, unwinding her long hair from the bun at her neck. She ran her fingers through it, loosening the few tangles, massaging her scalp. A bath sounded heavenly after her time skulking around the docks, but she needed the extra time to sleep more.

She dipped a rag in the now-tepid water in her basin and ran the cool cloth over her face and throat, then scrubbed both hands. Unlacing her front stays, she dropped the short brown corset into a chair, removed her dress, and lay down on top of the bed. She wouldn't get too comfortable. Anna-Marie needed to be up early.

***

Yelling woke Anna-Marie.

She sat straight up, reaching for the pocket watch on her bedside table, then sighed in relief. Good, she wasn't late. Yet.

As the bickering continued downstairs, Anna-Marie ignored it. Opening her large carpet bag, she rummaged around.

"Aha!" She donned her favorite pair of trousers. Anna-Marie had taken in all the seams so they fit perfectly. She tucked a dark shirt into the waistline, added her short, supple corset, the one without boning, and then her overskirt. Anna-Marie might like pants and their practicality for moving quickly, but she knew it was still a taboo fashion for women, regardless of how quickly it was catching on. So, for now, she would look the part of the respectable lady to attract as little attention as possible. At least, until they found the girls.

Her slender fingers made quick work of braiding her long hair. She coiled and pinned it out of the way and secured her sturdiest fascinator hat atop her head.

Next, a wide leather belt fitted with pouches slung low around her hips and her favorite spiked red boots over the top of her trouser legs. Anna-Marie was ready to go downstairs.

"You're lying!" Prudence stomped.

"Prove it." Vivien shrugged, unconcerned with the other girl's temper.

Anna-Marie rounded the banister and nearly collided with Patience, Prudence, and Vivien. Prudence and Vivien stood, glaring heatedly at each other. Patience was sitting on the floor with parts and pieces of Constantina's insides surrounding her, tinkering away.

"What is going on here?" Anna-Marie demanded.

Prudence spun toward her. "Vivien just came in. She was out all night and...Anna-Marie! You're back!"

Patience dusted off her hands and stood, careful not to get tangled in her skirt.

Anna-Marie made a mental note to offer the girl some trousers for their tinkering lessons. As much as she wanted to ask what she was doing with

Constantina at the moment, now wasn't the time. "Vivien, where were you last night?"

"Looking for you and the younger girls, of course." Vivien sniffed.

Anna-Marie tossed up her hands. She didn't believe it any more than Prudence, but Vivien and her nightlife were not the priority today. "As you can see, I'm back. Temperance and Rosie were stolen, and I don't have time for your quarrels if I'm to get them back. Do me a favor, please?" Though Vivien frowned, she didn't argue, and the other two nodded. "Stay in the house and don't kill each other. We may need to move quickly when I get back."

A scratching sound at the door caused all heads to turn. A folded scrap of paper drifted beneath the front door. Patience, being closest, scooped it up and handed it to Anna-Marie.

After unfolding the note, Anna-Marie scanned its contents quickly. "Change of plans. I need you all to gather your things. You're coming with me."

"What?"

"Where?"

"Pardon me?"

Anna-Marie let out her shrillest whistle. "When we retrieve the girls, we will very likely make enemies. Transportation out of the city is ready. I didn't expect it to be ready today, but it is."

Vivien crossed her arms and tilted her head. An assessing gaze roved over Anna-Marie. "You didn't say where we are going."

"We will travel by airship to Uncle Ernest's house in the country."

"You have an uncle?" Prudence's eyes widened. "Why did he leave you in the orphan house?"

"Airship?" Vivien brightened. "My parents took me on an airship once when I was a girl. I never thought I'd get to fly again."

Anna-Marie pulled out her pocket watch. The minutes were ticking. "Only bring what you cannot bear to leave behind."

Vivien surprised them all by going straight upstairs to pack.

Patience hurried after her.

"Well?" Anna-Marie raised an eyebrow at Prudence.

She ran her fingers through the ends of her auburn hair and shrugged. "I can bear to leave it all," Prudence said softly.

"Knock-knock!" Bert's chipper voice yelled from the direction of the dining hall.

Anna-Marie asked Prudence to straighten up the gears and wires Patience had left and then turned to her old friend. "I see you've let yourself in again."

Bert smiled without apology. "Couldn't shake the feeling that something was going on today. Is everyone all right? I overheard you mention leaving. Tell me it isn't so. Don't break me heart again," he said. clutching his sooty hat to his chest.

Anna-Marie rolled her eyes. "Oh, do be serious for a change. What brings you by, Bert?"

"There's talk all over the streets. More girls kidnapped. In broad daylight, the butcher says." Bert shook his head woefully. "It's terrible times. I came to warn you all to be careful."

Prudence piped up from down the hall where she'd been listening. "It's true! Tempy and Rosie were taken."

Anna-Marie shushed her with a quick look.

"Is that a fact?" Bert's frown deepened. "Is there anything I can do?"

"No, thank you." Anna-Marie shook her head. "We are in a bit of a hurry. You can understand I'd like to get the rest of the girls out of the city."

"When will you be back?"

"Goodbye, Bert." Anna-Marie squeezed his arm. "I really must be going." She watched as Bert, downcast, ambled back through the dining room and to the kitchen before she turned to pack her own things.

Her comb she retrieved from the parlor cushions, then up the stairs she went. Most of her belongings she'd never unpacked from the carpet bag. Shoving in a few garments, she took one last look around the room. Like Prudence, she wouldn't miss this place.

"Vivien," she called through the young woman's open door, "we need to be going."

"I'm almost finished."

Anna-Marie pushed the door wider. "Are you packing a trunk?" she asked in disbelief.

"Of course."

Anna-Marie gathered the last threads of her patience. "A bag. One that you can carry. That is all that you may bring."

"But…"

Anna-Marie stiffened her posture. "We will send for your trunk from Uncle Ernest's home. There is no possible way to bring it with us today, unless you mean to hoist it upon your back and lug it around the city yourself." She turned on her booted heel and stomped down the stairs to fetch her overcoat and umbrella. "We are leaving in exactly two minutes, with or without you."

They were a conspicuous lot, four young women laden with assorted bags, marching purposefully down alleyways as if they were strolling through Hyde Park.

Because Prudence didn't have a bag of her own, Anna-Marie tasked her with carrying her carpet bag. Best to have her hands free in case of incident.

The girls darted nervous glances and rushed to match paces. Nobody wanted to be the straggler in the group.

Anna-Marie had spotted the same hunched man behind them three times. He tried to disguise his pursuit as digging through garbage and scavenging, but she knew different. He was following them. She didn't mention him to the girls because she had an inkling he was there as a friend. Twice, he'd scared away young boys Anna-Marie knew to be pick-pockets.

She relaxed the grip on her umbrella slightly when a familiar door came into sight. As before, a shadow detached from the wall. This time, it was Cyrus himself.

"This way," he said.

Anna-Marie and the girls followed him to another street, where a steamer carriage waited.

Cyrus spoke to the driver who nodded. The hunched man appeared from the shadows and climbed aboard the rear of the vehicle.

"The girls will be taken to the airship and boarded to wait for us. The man you requested to meet is already there." Cyrus opened the door to the carriage.

Vivien simpered when Cyrus held a hand out to help her inside. She smiled and nodded, flouncing happily into the carriage.

Patience and Prudence clutched each other. "Anna-Marie, does he mean to say you aren't coming with us?"

Anna-Marie nodded, pretending she'd known the plan all along, acting as if she wasn't a bit nervous to send the girls alone to await her arrival when she wasn't even sure what today would bring for her or how long it would take to get the others back. "I will be with you as soon as we've gotten Temperance and Rosie back," she assured them. "Go on, scoot."

The moment the steam carriage rolled around the corner, she dropped the hand she'd been waving and turned on Cyrus. "How long is the pilot going to wait? Are you sure the girls will be safe?"

"I give you my word, they will be protected."

"Ha!" She clenched her umbrella. "Your word means nothing. We established last night you will lie for your own purposes."

"As for the pilot"—Cyrus ignored her barbs—"he has been paid handsomely to wait and promised more if he actually does so."

"Fine. Greed, I can trust." Anna-Marie tapped her foot on the dirty cobblestones. "Do we have a location for Temperance and Rosie?"

"Follow me."

Anna-Marie whipped her arm out and caught his sleeve. "I'm growing tired of those two words. Where are we going?"

Cyrus pulled her to him and spun against the wall of the nearest building. He leaned close, and Anna-Marie bit her lip to stop a shiver as he whispered, "The girls are in a factory near the Thames, just miles from where they were put on the boat last night. However, we don't want to spoil the surprise of our coming, and the streets have ears, as you know. If you can agree to ask questions later, I will let you go now." Cyrus waited a heartbeat. "If you would like to know more, by all means, I'm quite comfortable discussing it right now." He ran a finger down her cheek.

"Let's go." Anna-Marie pushed him away and straightened her overcoat.

Cyrus gave her a cheeky grin. "Oi, now you choose to be reasonable."

Chapter Eleven

"This is it?" Anna-Marie whispered.

Cyrus pointed. "Second building, red brick with the whitewash on the bottom."

Anna-Marie's stomach dropped. "You mean the one with every window boarded over and what looks like a whole corner of the roof gone?" The buildings before them were all ramshackle, abandoned or relocated when larger steam boats could no longer get to this smaller part of the river to export the goods.

"Yes." Cyrus answered.

Only two of his men had returned—the tall lanky man and the man whose niece was now inside the building. They had to assume the other man planned to betray them. Luckily, Cyrus confided even less in the men he hired than in Anna-Marie. The man wouldn't know they planned to rescue the girls, only that Cyrus needed a location of the man called Jack of all Traders.

The two silently studied the building and the surrounding area. Anna-Marie saw only one guard posted. He lounged in a doorway, smoking. She knew there were likely men inside, guarding the children. Anna-Marie wished she had a clue what to expect. What were they doing to the girls they abducted?

She needed to get a closer look.

Desperate, Anna-Marie looked at the building again. "Do you think they closed up the roof from the inside?" she whispered.

Cyrus squinted. "I can't tell, but I doubt it. After all, why go in through the roof when it's easier to kick down a few boards? Vagrants or thieves, they only look for the easy ways in, in my experience."

"Good." Anna-Marie shuffled from their hiding place into a side street that no longer faced the guard.

Cyrus followed. "Where are you going?"

"To the roof, of course." She bent and collected the hem of her skirt. In quick fashion, she had hooked two loops onto small buttons above her knees, revealing her trousers and allowing complete freedom of movement. "It would probably help if you distract the guard. Just in case."

A faint heat threatened to creep up her neck as Cyrus grunted at the word *distraction*, but she ducked her head to retrieve leather gloves from a pouch on her belt and busied herself putting them on as she gathered her composure. Now was not the time to ponder appreciative glances.

"The roof?" Cyrus said at last. "Do you plan to scale the building?" He raised one skeptical brow high, crossing his arms.

"No. Don't be ridiculous." Anna-Marie pushed open her umbrella. "I'm going to fly."

She pushed a small, concealed button on the handle of the umbrella. A whoosh sounded, and she felt warm air on her face. Quickly, she hurried down the street and around the corner to the backside of the factory she planned to enter. Right on time, as always—she approached the building, and her umbrella lifted higher, her arm straightening with it. Soon, her toes left the ground.

Up, up, she went.

Flying might have been an exaggeration. Floating, or drifting depending on wind currents, was the true function of her precious umbrella. Still, she would give almost anything to see the look on Cyrus's face right now.

As Anna-Marie drew even with the rooftop, she took a deep breath and focused on her task. Leaning, she carefully used her weight to bring the umbrella over a less crumbled section of roof, then slowly rolled her thumb down a tiny wheel on the umbrella shaft. This lowered the wick and extinguished the flame in the metal cannister, sealing the fuel shut. Her feet came to rest with a soft thud on solid ground, or roof.

Now, for the tricky part.

Anna-Marie knelt close to the hole's edge, but not so close she would tumble in if the building decided to crumble a bit more. She heard faint shouting from the street, probably Cyrus with her distraction. It was now or never.

From another pouch at her waist, Anna-Marie pulled a long cable. Thin but strong, she looped and tied one end around a chimney stack. The other end she dropped through the hole at the sturdiest-looking point. She could see machines and girls below. Her rope should take her down behind the large furnace. If nobody looked up and caught her, and if she didn't swing too close and get burned, she should be down in no time.

In retrospect, Anna-Marie decided "in no time" was a rather vague and incorrect estimate. Her arms ached from supporting her weight, and every few minutes, she had to stop and hang very still when one of the girls walked close to the corner where she was descending. Anna-Marie had also not factored in the difficulty of climbing with an umbrella clutched tightly beneath one's arm, but she had simply not been willing to leave it on the roof.

It was her favorite umbrella and would be quite inconvenient to replace. She already had a coat to repair.

Anna-Marie dropped the last three or four feet to the hard concrete floor. She stifled a groan as she stripped off her leather gloves and massaged her upper arms. Crouching behind a bale of cotton, Anna-Marie scanned the room, counting at least twenty-three girls. Some Chinese or Irish, immigrants judging by the distinct facial features or shock of red hair on numerous tiny frames. One thing the girls all had in common—size. They were all young or fairly small.

As a girl slipped carefully out from under a moving machine next to her, Anna-Marie understood. They wanted children who were little enough to fit between moving parts and pieces. Rather than shutting down machines for maintenance, these girls were being enslaved into dangerous duties to keep everything running constantly. She wondered if they even got more than a few hours of sleep a night.

Anger burned through her, aches and pains forgotten. As her eyes searched for Temperance and Rosie, Anna-Marie's mind scrambled for a plan. She hoped Cyrus was also coming up with something. Before she thought of anything she spotted one of the girls and heaved a breath of relief. Temperance was unharmed, at least.

She stole silently up to the machine where the girl was using some type of rod to try and clear blockage from between two oversized rollers.

"Psst." Anna-Marie hid behind a crate several feet away. "Tempy." She used the nickname she had heard the girls using at the orphan house and Temperance's head whipped toward her.

Anna-Marie motioned her over.

With a glance over both shoulders, Temperance quickly ran and ducked beside her, squeezing Anna-Marie's hands.

"You came!" she whispered loudly.

"I came. We have to get you out of here."

"I don't want to leave the others," Temperance whispered after Anna-Marie managed to sneak over and pull her away from the large rollers she was stationed at.

Rosie was a little further down the aisle, and Anna-Marie assumed the girl at her hip was the friend, Celia.

"We need to get you out of here before you're hurt or killed." Anna-Marie took the girl by the shoulders. "Go get Rosie and Celia before we're discovered. We can come back for the others."

"No." Temperance shook her head, her braid swinging violently. "You don't understand. They only use the girls here for a while. After they prove useful, they're moved to a whole new place to work. Anna-Marie"—Temperance's eyes filled with tears—"I heard them say they would move us tonight. If we don't get everyone out, they'll be gone."

"Fine. Let me think."

From the front of the building, yelling sounded. Cyrus pushed his way inside and demanded to see someone in charge. He was yelling about cheating, owed money, and generally causing a great scene.

Anna-Marie's gaze darted around the room. At the side, one window had two boards partially loosened. "Tell Rosie and Celia to spread out. Get as many girls who will leave and send them out that window. Temperance…" Anna-Marie held the younger girl's gaze. "If they won't leave, we don't have time to make them. I have a plan, but it could get us all killed just as easily as it could save us. Do you understand?"

"I understand."

"When everyone is out, yell, 'Fire!' loudly, then run like the dickens three blocks that way." Anna-Marie pointed the way she and Cyrus had come. "I'll find you."

Temperance ran, ducking low between machines. Soon, Rosie and Celia were running, tripping over tools and rags, scrambling to whisper hastily to every girl in the factory. Anna-Marie hoped they had enough time.

Now, for phase two.

Anna-Marie worked swiftly. She stuffed plenty of cotton into an overturned crate and sprinkled a line of black powder a little way from it, placing the crate as close as she dared to the room where Cyrus had been escorted—an office, she assumed.

With the strike of a match, she lit the little black line of gunpowder.

Next, she backtracked and opened the furnace door. Flames leapt inside. She measured the distance from the furnace to the open window where girls were climbing the sill. It would be close.

She plucked a rag from the floor. With a teaspoon from her hatband, she carefully transferred a heaping spoonful of gunpowder from the pouch on her belt to the rag, then tied it shut.

The men in the office noticed the fire outside their door just as the last three girls slipped through. Anna-Marie began inching toward the window herself. She needed to catch Cyrus's eye, but he was busy picking the pockets of the men trying to put out the fire.

They hadn't noticed the girls missing yet, but they would. And she still needed to warn Cyrus to get out.

There was nothing for it. Anna-Marie stood and marched to the window, ripping at the last boards blocking the opening. She would need a wider space than the children, anyway.

The noise caught everyone's attention.

"Hey! What do you think you're doing?" the guard yelled.

The other man stomped toward her. "How did you get in here?"

"Me?" Anna-Marie pretended confusion. "Do you have any idea who I am?"

"No."

"Good. Let's keep it that way." Anna-Marie picked up a splintered slat and swung with all her might.

The man wobbled but didn't go down. But Cyrus's large hands slamming him into the wall did the trick.

"Can you get these boards off?" Anna-Marie asked.

The second man pulled a pistol and fired. He was a bad shot, but Anna-Marie had no intention of giving him time to practice his aim. It was time to go.

Cyrus tugged Anna-Marie toward the back door, and with two stout kicks, it was open.

The man with the pistol was almost on them. A shot pelted into the wall inches from Anna-Marie.

"Wait!" she shouted at Cyrus. Anna-Marie raised her arm and threw the little rag bundle into the open furnace door. "Run!" In the next instant, she shoved Cyrus out, nearly tripping over her own umbrella. They ran hard but didn't escape the blast completely.

As gunpowder hit flames, the hot air expanded in the furnace, and the explosion rocked the already rickety factory. Bricks and boards flew outward.

Pain sliced across Anna-Marie's shoulder. She tripped and fell. Another blow landed across the back of her head.

"My umbrella," she muttered.

Then, everything faded to black.

Chapter Twelve

Anna-Marie awoke to the sensation of being bitten by ants. An army of them. She swiped at the offending insects, only to have a calloused hand catch her wrist. Her eyes shot open.

Cyrus shook his head. "Not yet."

"I'm sorry, ma'rm. I know it hurts like the blazes."

Anna-Marie blinked over her shoulder at the thin child currently running a needle and thread through her tender skin.

Temperance hovered nearby with worry-filled eyes.

Rosie, on the other hand, beamed and tugged her friend Celia over for introductions, as if Anna-Marie was not lying over Cyrus's lap with a ten-year-old stitching an open wound in her scandalously unclad shoulder.

"This is Celia. Celia, this is Anna-Marie. I told you she would come for us. She always comes back. She promised."

"Thank you." Celia scuffed her foot on the ground, not quite meeting Anna-Marie's eyes.

Anna-Marie gathered she might be shier than even Rosie had been.

Another prick of pain made her hiss, and all of the girls stepped back.

"Would someone like to tell me where we are and what's going on? We do have an airship to catch. What time is it? I can't reach my pocket watch."

"An airship!" Several girls nearby gasped. Others whispered.

"Singh is stitching you up," Temperance supplied helpfully. "It was her job to stitch up any of the girls who got hurt at the factory. Most of them even lived!"

Anna-Marie closed her eyes, suppressing a groan. She felt rather than heard Cyrus chuckle, but when she glared up at him, he donned an innocent mask of calm.

"We are far enough away from the factory to avoid notice," he assured her. "You were losing too much blood. Plus, you're hard to carry with that umbrella and those blasted boots trying to stab a man at every turn."

"All done." Singh tied the thread. She bit it clean with her teeth, making Anna-Marie sad that such a task didn't phase the child for a second. She should be playing "doctor" on dolls, not performing surgeries in the street.

Making as dignified an exit as possible from Cyrus's legs, Anna-Marie turned to the little girl. "Thank you, Singh." She clasped the child's hand with her good arm and squeezed. "I truly appreciate it."

"'Twas nothin'."

"Let's play a game!" Anna-Marie smiled at the scared and suspicious faces surrounding her. To be honest, the fact they were all still here and not scattered to the winds, each running off to fend for themselves, was a miracle. "Follow the leader. The first leader shall take us all the way to that collapsed cart, there." She pointed. "Then, I shall pick another."

The children fell into line naturally behind the tallest girl. As they all marched or skipped away, Anna-Marie's fingers flew through her pockets. Once a quick inventory of her person and belongings was complete, she set off after the children.

Cyrus matched her pace. "I have one question."

"I'm okay. It'll stop hurting eventually."

"That wasn't my question."

"Oh." Anna-Marie turned her head to look at him.

He smirked. "What did you throw in that furnace?"

Anna-Marie lifted one shoulder. "Nothing much. Just a spoonful of gunpowder."

She left Cyrus staring after her, both eyebrows raised, as she quickened her steps. With a giant smile, feeling lighter than a person on the run after recently blowing up a building should be allowed to feel, she scooped up the tiniest straggler in their odd party and joined the game of follow the leader. Before long, she was leading the girls around a bend in the Thames.

The river widened, and there, right where Cyrus promised it would be, was a mid-sized boat. Steam was chugging from its chimney and it had not one but two large paddle wheels on the back. Anna-Marie cocked her head to study the sides of the boat, startled when she realized the long metal apparatuses on each side were long guns. Just what type of boat were they boarding?

She stood aside while Cyrus had a quick conversation with the captain. Another man appeared on deck. Beside her, a squeal escaped the little girl whose finery had become grungy and torn in the last day. She rushed to the gangplank, where her uncle caught her in his arms and spun her around.

Cyrus placed a hand on the man's shoulder, nodding. It appeared the debt was forgiven, as promised.

"All aboard!" The captain called.

Anna-Marie and Cyrus helped the girls navigate the rough plank of wood and then the stairs descending below the deck.

"Best to stay out of sight until we reach the airship towers," Cyrus said.

"Agreed."

The steamboat's engine made a whooshing noise as someone fed the firebox that heated the boiler and the boat got underway. In minutes, the group of children were asleep, exhaustion claiming each of them.

"I'm glad that's over." Anna-Marie raised and lowered her arm, testing the stitches and the pain. Her shoulder had subsided into a deep throb, and her head ached.

"It's never over," Cyrus murmured.

At least, she thought he murmured it. Things were getting hazy. Her eyes were heavy—so heavy. Perhaps she should rest with the girls.

Cyrus snapped his fingers beneath her nose.

She blinked rapidly. "What?"

"I said you have to stay awake." Cyrus turned her to face away from him.

Before she could protest, he was running his fingers through her hair. Anna-Marie stiffened. As quickly as it began, the touch disappeared.

"You have a lump on your head. I think it was a brick that knocked you out, but what with runnin' and duckin' for my life and all when some woman blasted a building down almost on top of me without warning, I didn't see for sure." Cyrus tugged her to face him again. "You have to stay awake. I've heard of men dying when they go to sleep after a head injury."

"I'm sure it isn't so bad." Anna-Marie shook her head, then winced as the throbbing in her head surged above the aching in her shoulder.

Gingerly, she touched the back of her head. There was a lump, indeed. She sighed.

"How do you propose I stay awake when this boat is rocking me to sleep?" Anna-Marie caught the smirk just before Cyrus opened his mouth. She held up a hand. "Scratch that. I'll take myself for a stroll on the deck."

"Suit yourself." Cyrus shrugged. "If you need other ideas, I'll be here."

Anna-Marie nodded to the captain as she passed on her way to the rail. The sights weren't exactly inspiring. Murky river water. Dilapidated houses. It was only far in the distance that the landscape began to change.

It was subtle at first. Neat rowhouses appeared. Then, larger expanses of green grass lined the banks. The factories and boat building houses rose, tall and sturdy, unlike the dilapidated area they had recently fled.

And then there were the towers. Great docks in the sky. The Queen's flags fluttered in the evening breeze. And even in the moonlight, airships could be seen tethered to the massive structures high above them.

Anna-Marie gave the vessels one long look, then descended into the bowls of their little boat to wake the girls.

It grew darker and darker as she took each step down. The pounding in her head made her vision swim. As the boat bumped alongside the dock, Anna-Marie stumbled from the impact and tried to catch herself. The boat bumped again, harder this time, slamming her into the wall. She couldn't take another step.

Deciding it would be best to sit and rest until the boat was secured and unmoving, she sank down, sitting with her head on her knees. Drowsiness she'd been denying caught up, and she sank into slumber.

Chapter Thirteen

Anna-Marie sat up.

She was in a bed, which was startling enough, but more surprisingly, the bed was clean and plush and felt like heaven, and she wasn't sure she wanted to leave it at all.

Still, her practical side won out. Anna-Marie acknowledged she'd never had so soft a bed in her life, and it was located in a room she definitely didn't recognize. A peek under the covers confirmed she was dressed only in a shift. Warm and comfortable though she might feel, that wasn't enough to mean she wasn't in jeopardy. Or the girls!

The last thing she remembered was the girls and the boat. She was going to wake them. Everything after that simply came and went through her memory in uncomfortable flashes. Being slapped in the face. The continued pulsating pain flaring and dimming, flaring and dimming in her head with each step. But the steps couldn't have been hers. She distinctly remembered being jostled and cursed at once or twice and the sensation of thick arms wrapped around her.

That begged the questions, how long had she been unconscious, and where had she been carried to?

Anna-Marie stood to stretch, assessing herself. Her mouth tasted like old cotton, but her head was no longer throbbing, thankfully. The same couldn't be said for her shoulder.

She twisted her neck to look at the wound and winced from not only the pain, but from the sight. Red, inflamed skin was squished and pinched between the stitches. She counted them—eight stitches. A pink sluice was dripping down from the wound, slowly.

If her arm was sliced open so badly, she hated to think of the hole in her poor overcoat. A shame, as it had been her favorite. Maybe she would be able to repair the hole. If not, there was clearly no need to replace all of the buttons she had sacrificed during the pursuit of the kidnapped girls.

Before she had more time to dwell on the state of her clothes, much less look for them, the knob on the door turned, and a man entered.

"Oh! You're awake. That's good then, isn't it?"

He was dressed in a white shirt with the laces loose at the neck. The fabric had possibly been crisp at some point in its life, but it was now wrinkled enough to give the impression of having been wadded up before the owner donned it. Rough leather breeches, from which spyglasses of various lengths hung, sat on his hips. The man nudged the door open fully with one foot. His tall brown boots were polished and made of fine leather, a stark contrast to the rest of the ensemble.

Anna-Marie's gaze traveled upward again. His arms were laden with a tray.

Her stomach growled. She was prepared to forgive the man's intrusion, until he came closer and she saw the tray he carried contained rags, water, strips of cloth, and a handful of large leaves. No food whatsoever.

"You again? What, no oranges?" she asked.

The man placed the tray on a desk, the only other piece of furniture besides the bed, and turned.

"We may not have exchanged names but I'd rather flattered myself that you would know who I am, since I found out you requested me personally for this trip." He bowed. "Ambrose

Banks. At your service. You are currently in my cabin."

Anna-Marie's pulse quickened. Surely, Cyrus hadn't tricked her. Sold her to this man or betrayed her and the girls.

"I didn't expect a crewman tasked with tidying the cargo hold to rank high enough up to have his own cabin." She narrowed her eyes. "But if this is your cabin, why am I in it precisely?"

"What do you say we forget that we were both hiding out in the cargo hold, you as a stowaway and me from my crew who had not yet acclimated to my presence, and begin fresh. As to the cabin, you were out cold. Result of that head injury, if I had to guess. Bloke that brought you here threatened to burn my whole bloody airship if you weren't taken care of, so I've undertaken the task of your well-being." Banks held up the obvious tray of medical supplies between them. "*Infamous Inheritance* is not only my most-prized, but also my sole possession. I'd rather not lose her, you understand. In that regard, let's get on with the whole 'me saving your life' bit. As much as I'm thoroughly enjoying having this conversation with you, having your nightdress draped fetchingly over your…well…all of you…" His gaze traveled from her hair to her bare toes and back again before he swallowed. "It would make my job a load easier if you were to get back in bed and let me apply this salve and eucalyptus leaves to that gash on your shoulder."

While Anna-Marie was not ashamed of her body, she didn't relish having it on display for a basic stranger either. At the same time, she felt she would be at quite a disadvantage, lying in the bed versus standing to meet this man head on if he tried to overpower her.

"Saving my life?" She quirked a thin brow, deciding for the moment to focus on one bit of Banks' ramblings at a time. "I may not be fit as a fiddle, but I assure you, sir, neither am I on death's door."

"Not *sir*. Call me Ambrose, call me Banks, call me 'you there', call me the most handsome man you've ever seen, call me juggler of oranges if you wish, call me whatever you please, but *sir* was reserved for my father, and I'd just as soon not think of him." Banks grimaced. "And as for death's door, well, you may not be laying on the doorstep, but it is a short path if an infection sets in. Trust me." His eyes shuttered, and for one moment, his open face was guarded. He visibly shook himself and smiled again. "And I'd hate for you to die before solving the mystery of why you wished to see me in the first place. I've quite a ravenous sort of curiosity, too curious for my own good, most would say. It would be spiteful to die and leave my curiosity piqued."

Anna-Marie didn't know what to make of the loose-tongued man in front of her. He was handsome in a classical, perfectly symmetrical face, chiseled cheekbones, and tousled hair kind of way. And that hair. It was the color of sun-warmed straw. Even plainly dressed as he was, everything about this man was bright. He was so…exuberant, cheerful even. She'd spent a lifetime with tired, sour, or plain old mean individuals. Cheerful was new.

"Just get it over with." She turned, sliding her nightgown further down her arm to give him access to her shoulder, while scanning the room for her umbrella or any other weapon, in case she needed one.

Banks blushed—actually blushed—when she bared her shoulder and back to him instead of climbing into the bed and hiding beneath the blankets.

"Warm in here, isn't it," he murmured.

Anna-Marie felt a bit stifled, but she didn't think it was enough to account for the heat in the man's cheeks. She was flummoxed by his reaction. Was he embarrassed? Affected by her scant amount of covering? Upset at her lack of propriety?

While she mulled over the possibilities, Banks finished his task with clinical precision and far more care and gentleness than the little surgeon who'd stitched her had been able to impart.

The soft whisper of his fingertips lulled her and awoke her at the same time. It was tempting, oh so tempting, to relax into his ministrations and close her eyes, relishing this feeling of being cared for—a feeling she couldn't recall having before. She took a deep breath to shake off the feeling. It was a mistake. At once, the scent of bergamot and rosemary mixed with cedar assailed her. It was such a fresh yet masculine scent, and it took her completely by surprise. She wanted to inhale again, fill her nose with it, with him.

When Cyrus looked at her or bantered with her or, goodness forbid, touched her, he was heat and danger, a challenge to her system, and a puzzle to solve

But this, this was different. It was warm, unexpected, and…vulnerable.

Her wayward thoughts caused her to snap peevishly, "Where did Cyrus go?"

"I haven't the faintest clue, nor was I interested in prologuing my acquaintance with the bloke to find out. He did leave a note for you."

"Oh?"

"Here, let me find it."

Banks reached in his breeches pocket and retrieved a small parchment. Hastily scrawled, the note was vague and curt, precisely like one would expect from a known scoundrel who would abandon a woman in a weakened state.

"Jack wasn't there. Gone to find him. You still owe me payment. I plan to collect."

Anna-Marie sighed. It was for the best. She knew Cyrus for what he was, used him for what he was, and had never expected him to help them make the journey to Uncle Ernest's home. Still, she'd expected more than being dumped unceremoniously on the ship, unconscious to boot.

She did hope he caught up to Jack of All Traders, though. That man needed to be put out of business. Permanently. If anyone could find him, it would be Cyrus. And she had no pity for the child-snatching blackguard when he did.

Banks cleared his throat.

Anna-Marie looked up from the parchment and frowned. The man was doing his utter best not to stare at her again.

"Is there anything else you need?"

"My clothes."

"I seem to remember suggesting that some time ago." His voice was refined, velvety, but

Anna-Marie detected a sarcastic undertone she found all too appealing.

She crossed her arms. "Yes, well, they appear to be missing. Not much I can do about that, now is there?"

"Missing?" He looked around the room, not able to stop himself from glancing down Anna-Marie's slender form again. "Ah. One of the girls did ask about laundry. They must have decided to wash them for you. If you'll allow me…" He brushed against her in the confines of the small space as he stepped past her and to a thin door, a panel really, unnoticeable in the wall. When he pressed, it slid open with the slightest *whoosh*, and Anna-Marie was impressed. Steam-operated secret rooms. Perhaps there was more to this good-humored man than met the eye.

"Here we are." He presented Anna-Marie with a long brown coat adorned with gold trim and gold buttons. "It will be a bit large, but it should work temporarily."

A captain's coat.

"You're the captain?" She didn't bother to hide the surprise in her voice. "So this really is your ship?" She had not detected a lie when he said it was his most prized possession but she was still struggling to take it all in. Another thing to blame on the head injury, she decided.

Captain Ambrose Banks bowed with a flourish. "At your service. Isn't that why you requested me?"

"Anna-Marie, Anna-Marie!"

The shouts outside of the door drew Captain Banks up tall.

Anna-Marie, too, hastily slid her arms into the coat and pulled it closed. She crossed the room and pulled the door open. "Whatever is the matter?" she asked the yelling girls.

Prudence was flushed, and she bent over to catch her breath. Even Patience looked disheveled, though she carefully tucked loose strands of hair behind her ear and didn't look as if she had run the whole way.

"We heard you were injured," Patience said.

Prudence straightened and nodded. "Are you okay? Where is Cyrus? Temperance said you blew up a building!"

Anna-Marie felt more than heard Captain Banks step up behind her. She could only assume he heard the remark, and she stifled a smirk as she imagined the shocked look on his expressive face, finding out he was caring for a woman who blew things up, allegedly.

"Yes, well." She ignored the building comment for now. "As you can see, I'm in tip top shape."

"What are you wearing?" Patience asked.

"The captain was kind enough to loan me a coat. Would you girls be kind enough to check on Temperance and my laundry? I'd very much like to get dressed in my own clothes." It was unsettling how the long, heavy coat warmed her inside and out.

Patience and Prudence bobbed their heads and left to find Temperance.

The voice that rang out next was male and agitated. "Captain!"

"Duty calls." Banks strode to the hidden closet once more, donned a coat nearly matching the one he had given Anna-Marie—navy with silver this time—and a gray aviator's cap, complete with goggles, silver metal studs, and a thin gold rope tied in nautical knots around the brim.

Anna-Marie snorted. "No pirate's hat? With a ship called the *Infamous Inheritance*, I expected something more theatrical."

Banks only shrugged. "I'm afraid they were all out of pirate hats when I called at the tailor to have my pilot's outfits made."

"Of course," she deadpanned. His tone was so matter-of-fact that Anna-Marie didn't know if he was being serious or sarcastic. She rolled her eyes as she watched Captain Banks stroll from the cabin and take the stairs up to the deck two at a time, heckling the man who called for him along the way.

Anna-Marie was pleased to see several familiar young faces appear from down the opposite end of the corridor. The girls all carried various pieces of her ensemble bundled in their arms. She released a heavy breath when she saw her hat and umbrella among the articles. Anna-Marie would need to do a better job of staying conscious, if only to keep up with her accessories in the future.

She ushered the girls inside.

"Oh, go on," Anna-Marie told them, noticing the jaw-dropped stares at the plush bed in the corner.

With giggles and no small amount of pushing and shoving, Temperance, Patience, Prudence, Rosie, and Celia all piled onto the bed. *At least now, only the bed is crowded and not the whole tiny cabin*, Anna-Marie thought wryly.

She dropped the large coat onto the desk, not willing to open the secret closet in front of the girls. As she donned her pants, blouse, corset, and overskirt, she listened to the girls' chatter.

"I can't believe we got out of that factory."

"She blew up a building."

"I can't believe we get to fly."

"It's his first flight."

"Do you think we'll all crash?"

Anna-Marie honed in on the last two comments. "Whose first flight?"

"The captain," Rosie piped up. "I heard the crew say he'd never flown before. Two men walked right off the ship. They took that steam elevator contraption down to the docks, but I heard them say they'd rather starve than work on a ship full of unlucky women passengers and a bored noble playin' at bein' a pilot."

The superstition that women onboard a ship, in the sea or the air, was one Anna-Marie was familiar with—she paid it no attention. The captain never flying a ship before, however, was news she wished she'd known. Perhaps before they'd boarded.

Her shoulder ached by the time she finished dressing, but she noticed it was a dull ache, much fainter than before. She made a mental note to ask what had been in the salve, though if she had to guess, one of the ingredients must be a numbing agent.

"I believe we should go above deck."

The girls all groaned. Anna-Marie simply pointed one slender finger at the door.

"Spit spot, I'd like a tour of this ship, and you all have lazed about long enough. I'd like to see the other girls as well." Anna-Marie would not be able to rid herself of the tension coiled in her neck until she knew everyone was truly safe. She might not have sensed a threat from Captain Banks, but that didn't mean the rest of the crew could be trusted. The children were her responsibility now, and she would brook no more harm coming to a single one of them. She pinned her hat in place and hung her umbrella over the crook in her arm.

Patience slipped into the lead, with Rosie and Celia next, followed by Prudence. Anna-Marie smiled at the way the older girls had also clearly taken it upon themselves to shepherd the younger two. Temperance walked next to Anna-Marie.

"Where is Vivien?" Anna-Marie asked. She was not surprised she hadn't seen the older, angrier girl yet. And she wasn't even surprised when Temperance answered.

"She didn't come with us."

Anna-Marie had begun to suspect as much.

Temperance continued as if asked. "She got out of the carriage when we were slowed in traffic. I haven't seen her since. Probably went back to get her dumb trunk."

They were climbing the last three steps, the other girls already waiting on the deck, when haughty yelling could be heard. The individual barking orders had no regard for those around them—that was obvious.

Anna-Marie frowned.

Temperance ran the last few steps. Anna-Marie reached the deck, and her eyes went directly to the source of noise, though she didn't need to look to recognize that voice.

Vivien.

Raking her windblown hair from her face, Vivien glared at the deckhand lounging against the rail. "I said that I need this trunk taken to my cabin. Now."

Unphased, the man shook his head. "I don't know who you are, lady. It's up to the captain if you get on this boat or not. Even if you are, there aren't any cabins to put that trunk in. It goes in the cargo hold with everything else."

"Ughh!" Vivien stomped and placed both hands on her ample hips. She turned her angry gaze on the rest of the ship, eyes scanning for the captain or someone who she could threaten into doing what she wanted.

Anna-Marie closed her eyes a moment, listening to the sounds around her: numerous girls rushing around the deck, *oohing* and *ahhing* over new sights; crewmen calling out to one another as they readied the airship; the cawing of sea birds around them; and waves lapping the docks far below the tower to which they were tethered in the air. Anything to block out the screeching of Vivien. She opened her eyes and sighed the moment Vivien spotted her.

The young woman's eyes narrowed and then brightened, a false smile spreading across her face. "Anna-Marie! Please tell this oaf that I'm with you. He is refusing to load my trunk."

Giving the man a tight smile, Anna-Marie asked him to give them a moment. He happily vacated the railing and joined two other men coiling ropes.

When he was out of earshot, Anna-Marie turned back to Vivien. "You mean, the trunk I specifically told you not to bring? The trunk you apparently abandoned the carriage and other girls to go and get?"

Vivien's fake smile pulled down into an arrogant scowl.

Before either woman could say another word, a clamoring sounded behind them. Anna-Marie moved past Vivien to watch as the elevator rose slowly into view. Ironworks decorated the exterior in scrolling filigree patterns. She stepped to the rail and leaned over, clucking her tongue in disappointment when the fog was too thick to see the base of the pulley system.

"Steam-powered engine."

Anna-Marie hadn't even heard Captain Banks approach over the racket of the elevator next to her. "Oh?"

"That is what you wanted to know, isn't it? Whether it was hand-operated or steam-powered?"

"Perhaps I was simply considering the merits of flinging myself overboard rather than going on a maiden voyage with an inexperienced pilot." Anna-Marie lifted one eyebrow, turning to face him.

"Found that out, did you?"

He didn't bother to lie or try to embellish his experience. Anna-Marie didn't know if she should be impressed or wary.

"If you plan to toss yourself over, I suggest waiting to see if I prove to be a surprisingly good captain first. After all, if I'm terrible, you'll still be able to jump overboard while we're in the air," Banks continued, as if discussing nothing more important than the weather. "Who knows, if we're too far off course, you might even be over the ocean. I would personally prefer to jump into the sea than into a sea of people. Better view, too, away from all the fog. And if by chance I'm a decent pilot, you have the option of not jumping and arriving safely at your destination."

"I suppose I shall take your advice. After all, I can't in good conscience leave thirty girls in your care."

At that, his eyes did bulge. "No. Definitely not. Then, I might have to jump as well."

Anna-Marie surprised herself by laughing.

"I haven't heard that laugh in a good many years."

Anna-Marie's gaze jerked to the side. Striding from the elevator came Bert with Constantina in tow.

Anna-Marie excused herself and made her way the short distance to Bert, but not before Vivien launched herself at him.

"Oh! Thank you again for bringing my trunk. I would have died to leave it behind!" Vivien clung to his arm.

Bert grinned. "Happy to be of help."

"Please, won't you come with us?" Vivien blinked her long eyelashes at him, mouth set in a seductive pout.

"I've got customers to see to. Can't have half of London goin' cold without their coal, ya know."

Anna-Marie interrupted. "I see you've brought Constantina, as well."

Bert extracted himself gently from Vivien under the pretense of lifting the medium automaton. "I already had a wagon loaded. Figured she was just one more thing to bring."

Anna-Marie noticed the way he said *she* and not *it* to refer to the automaton. Bert was one of the few people who knew how much Constantina really meant to her. He had helped her scavenge so many of the pieces. They had made an adventure of it, and he had seen Anna-Marie focus all her energy on only Constantina every time she received a beating or narrowly escaped worse. He had caught her whispering her plans for revenge to Constantina more than once, and he never teased her or told anyone. Constantina had been her first friend, followed by Bert. Eventually, she had come to consider the girls family too. And then Anna-Marie had left without so much as a goodbye.

In her defense, there hadn't been a choice or time for goodbyes. Not once Cyrus had taken her. But they didn't know that.

As if thinking along the same lines, Bert winked. "Couldn't let you go without a proper goodbye this time."

She looked into Bert's eyes now and saw something like regret. He quickly masked it and placed a kiss on each of her cheeks.

Vivien pulled Bert's arm, turning him to her, then kissed him hard on the lips. "That's a proper goodbye." She leveled a stormy gaze at Anna-Marie and then flounced away to harass another crewman about her trunk.

Last call for the elevator descending went out, and Bert hopped on just in the nick of time.

"Friend of yours?" Captain Banks asked.

Anna-Marie decided to pretend she thought he was referring to Vivien. "She is another of the girls that I'm trying to take to a new life. If she heard you refer to us as friends, I'm afraid you wouldn't have to jump overboard. She'd undoubtedly push you."

Banks nodded. "Duly noted."

"Are you the captain?" Vivien spotted him then. She simpered. "I'm so exhausted. Would you mind showing me to my cabin? Your men refuse to take my trunk there or show me where it is."

"The men are correct. The trunk goes in the cargo hold."

"But—"

Captain Banks held up a hand. "And you will be bunking with the other girls in a space beside it. So, you see, it's almost like your trunk will be in your cabin after all." He made a gesture at the closest man, who gave a nod and hoisted the trunk over one shoulder.

Sputtering, Vivien watched him go and then turned back to the captain. "Surely there is a cabin somewhere I can use? I'm not a regular orphan like these other street rats."

Banks crossed his arms. "I'm sorry. The only cabin is mine, and it is currently occupied."

Vivien's eyes grew the size of dinner rolls. She looked between Captain Banks and Anna-Marie before letting out a strangled noise and stomping away to sulk below deck.

"I'm perfectly happy to reside with the girls," Anna-Marie said.

Captain Banks drew himself up taller. "And risk collapsing back into unconsciousness or an infection from the damp? With the *Infamous Inheritance* at risk? I think not! I will simply have to endure sharing my cabin until you disembark healed and whole." His light blue eyes twinkled as he spoke.

"How gallant." Anna-Marie's lips twisted in a smirk. "And my reputation?"

"Fret not. I'm certain my reputation will be safe from your, shall we say, less than desirable one, blown-up buildings included." Banks grinned. "There is one question I must ask."

"Oh?" Anna-Marie leaned casually against the railing.

"Where are we flying to?"

"You're the captain," Anna-Marie spluttered.

"Yes, but your first charming friend, the bloke that dropped you in my cabin like a sack of potatoes, was a bit reticent when he booked your passage. He told me only that you needed a ship and had requested me. There was no mention of thirty young girls, I might add, but that is neither here nor there."

Anna-Marie hedged. "You didn't ask where you would be flying this ship?"

"It didn't seem important with a heavy bag of coins in my hands. Besides, he wouldn't speak of the destination, and I'm not a pushy gentleman, so, as my crew would like to know—and I'd rather them not catch on that I haven't the faintest clue— I ask you again…Where can we fly you today, woman of such mystery?"

Perhaps this trip would be more interesting than she imagined. If the cheery captain could indeed fly them without incident, that is. She half-worried he would treat flying as jokingly as he seemed to treat everything.

"Frinton-on-Sea," she said.

"Somewhere I've never been."

"Is that a problem?" Anna-Marie narrowed her eyes.

"Quite the opposite. It's an adventure!" Captain Ambrose Banks walked away, whistling a tune.

Chapter Fourteen

By evening, it was clear to see that many of the girls were sick from the constant motion of the airship.

Endless excitement over the novelty of being high in the sky held aloft by an enormous balloon above the center of the ship soon turned to green faces and cries of agony rather than awe. Vivien was not immune to the illness.

"I said, get me a rag!" Vivien yelled at one of the younger girls, unleashing her ire as frequently as she emptied her stomach into a bucket.

The girl stumbled, running to do as she was told. Anna-Marie placed a hand on her shoulder when the girl stepped down into the large, roped off 'room' below deck, where makeshift pallets had been made from old sails and whatever other cloth could be sacrificed. She knelt and dried the girl's tears, then sent her above deck for fresh air.

"Leave Vivien to me." She winked.

Bearing a fresh stack of rags—torn cloth from an old blouse in her own carpet bag, which she'd finally located in a stack of cargo—Anna-Marie placed the pile in the center of the room. A few girls snatched one up to wipe their mouths. Others stayed groaning where they lay.

Anna-Marie knelt next to Vivien's feet in order to stay away from the contents of the bucket near her head. "Vivien."

"Go away," she muttered.

"I thought you'd like to know we will arrive by mid-morning tomorrow." She'd gotten this information from a man who was comparing landmarks below to the map in hand as a means to track their progress. "In the meantime, these girls are not your servants." Anna-Marie's tone was sickly sweet, steel seeping through it. "Rags are over there, if you need one."

Anna-Marie stood and surveyed the rest of the room. She counted thirty-two pallets. Eleven girls were sick, including Celia, and three were huddled together, looking scared and suspicious. Four more were sleeping, and with Rosie seated next to Celia to offer comfort, that left thirteen girls exploring the ship. She spoke to the girls who were awake, promising to see if there was anything she could find to ease their sickness and return later.

Though the motion sickness wasn't affecting her personally, she couldn't help the relief when she stepped onto the deck and into the open air once again. She didn't like confined places. Cyrus hadn't mentioned they would be boarding such a small airship. Then again, she hadn't asked many questions, since her goal was only to find the heir of Lucifer Banks.

It was time for the conversation she needed to have with him.

The wind picked up, and Anna-Marie steadied her hat, which threatened to blow away despite her hat pins. She looked at the flurry of activity as men adjusted sandbags and ropes, trying to offset the tilt of the ship. Past them, she spotted the captain at the helm. He was rapidly calling out orders while studying a compass.

A sail out in front of the balloon was rolled up. An odd wing-like sail at the rear of the ship opened, and Captain Banks adjusted it like a rudder, steering the ship back into a stream of air that would take them forward, instead of off their trajectory.

Anna-Marie was fascinated by all of it but also by the man himself. She took advantage of his engaged attention to study him. His captain's coat had been tossed aside, his sleeves rolled up and showing tanned, leanly muscled arms. His hat was slightly askew yet looked jaunty enough to match his ear-to-ear grin. The man was straining to keep the tail-rudder in place and laughing the entire time, while men across the ship were yelling or cursing the presence of the women as being responsible for an impending storm. One or two crossed themselves as if preparing for doom. But Banks appeared to be having the time of his life.

Anna-Marie narrowed her eyes at him. Maybe he really was playing nursemaid on the sheer desire not to lose his ship. He clearly loved the darned thing. And she felt jealous. Not of the airship, per se, but of Banks's ability to be so wholeheartedly and unabashedly joyous. Free.

She longed for that feeling in a way she didn't even realize was possible. Freeing the girls from the orphan house had been her goal. And then freeing the girls from the factory. She even hoped in time to free them and herself from Uncle Ernest. But free to pursue something for the fun of it? Even tinkering, which she loved, typically served a purpose. She hadn't dared to imagine such a possibility as simply doing as she pleased for the pleasure of it. And now, Banks was making her want that very thing.

"Anna-Marie," he said with a start. "Give me a hand?"

She accepted the compass with a nod, as if she hadn't been staring at him for the last several minutes. Banks used two hands to wrench the lever for the rudder. The ship shuddered and then jumped forward before settling back into a gentle glide.

"Why were you hiding in the cargo hold when we met?"

"It was my first day as captain. Not everyone was happy with the new arrangement." He raised both hands in a 'can you believe it' gesture. "Since I didn't know a thing about being captain anyway, I decided to give them their space."

Anna-Marie looked at the sky around them, noticing the graying clouds. So, Cyrus had not been exaggerating about an inexperienced airship captain. "Will you have time to talk before we get to Frinton-on-Sea?" she asked. "Or will your captain's duties keep you here for the duration?"

"Once we're out of this weather, a crewman can take over for me."

Anna-Marie nodded. She tried not to appear anxious, but clearly failed.

Mistaking her look for concern over the weather, Banks assured her it was nothing. "We'll be out of this in no time, I'm certain. It's given us speed, too, which means we'll be at Frinton-on-Sea in time for a late breakfast."

Anna-Marie frowned, not only because he'd barely ever flown before and, therefore, all his certainty about the weather was empty chatter to make her feel better, but also because a shorter trip meant even less time to convince Banks of what she wanted him to do, what the girls needed him to do.

Deciding there was nothing to be done about it at the moment, and praying Banks was a fast learner, Anna-Marie strolled the deck. She kept far from the rails. The ship pitching back and forth was enough to remind her to be cautious, flying umbrella or not.

Anna-Marie mulled over her next steps as she paced. She would confront Banks about the neglect of the orphanage, obviously. Her original plan had been to confront his father in some large, public venue where embarrassment would cause him to recommit finances to the place and the girls. Having met the younger Banks, she considered the best approach. He seemed congenial enough. His crew respected him. Perhaps he would be more reasonable than his father.

The wind blew harder. The third time Anna-Marie nearly lost her hat, she pulled out her pocket watch. Time for tea. She doubted any of the men were going to see to a proper afternoon tea, but if she could find a kitchen, she could sort it out.

~

"Rosie, we do not slurp. We sip."

Anna-Marie pursed her lips sternly. She might have only found a mixture of tankards, tea cups, and wine glasses in the small kitchen cupboards, but she would not see the girls behave like the men who normally drank from them. When Rosie lifted a pinkie and took a delicate sip of tea from her large mug, Anna-Marie nodded. Girls around them chuckled until one strict look silenced them.

"Anna-Marie?"

"Yes, Temperance?"

"Why do you always insist on tea at the exact time?" Her fingers claimed a small slice of toast as she asked. She shoved it in her mouth without waiting for an answer.

"Teatime is halfway between lunch and dinner. Not only is it relaxing, but it is practical. We cannot be expected to have half the energy we need to go about our day if we are starving. Thus, tea." Anna-Marie sipped from her own teacup.

"We rarely had tea at the orphan house after you left," Prudence said softly. "I'd forgotten how nice it was."

"Anna-Marie, will you tell us where we're going again? Your uncle?" Patience lowered her voice. "Will he let all of these other girls stay too."

The ship listed sharply to the left. Anna-Marie finished her tea in one swallow—one dainty swallow, of course. She couldn't abide spilling tea, and the weather clearly intended for them to spill everything before this journey finished. Anna-Marie looked each of the girls in the eye, thinking carefully before she answered Patience.

"Uncle Ernest is a title, not an actual relation."

The faces in front of her displayed various degrees of surprise and wariness. Good. Uncle Ernest was a better fate than most, but she wouldn't lie to them.

"He provides warm lodging, good food, and lessons such as needlework, cooking, even reading and penmanship in exceptional cases. In return, you...we...work for Uncle Ernest. He likes information. In some instances, that information is best obtained by a servant or companion living in the house. Someone like us."

"We're still slaves, then." Rosie crossed her thin arms over her chest.

Anna-Marie understood her feelings very well. It wasn't ideal. "We will be fed and cared for, and I assure you, not a soul will lay a hand on you. Uncle Ernest doesn't believe in that kind of work for girls. He is greedy but not completely heartless."

The ship bobbed and dipped. Several girls on pallets groaned or cried out.

"I need to go see how things are above the deck. Girls, let's not tell everyone about Uncle Ernest yet. I promise, I'm working on a way out. Until then, phase one teaches lessons that can do nothing but improve your stations and theirs. Let's not discuss phase two unless I fail to secure our release."

Prudence nodded.

Rosie sniffed but mumbled an unhappy okay.

The other girls agreed.

Anna-Marie stood and shook out her overskirt. She gained half the steps before the next gust of wind crashed into the ship. Suddenly, shouts sounded overhead. Her stomach leapt into her throat.

The airship was dropping.

Rapidly.

Chapter Fifteen

Anna-Marie fought to control the sick feeling inside of her. She desperately wanted to go up on deck and find out what was happening, but as their descent showed no signs of slowing, she knew her first priority had to be the girls.

"Patience!" she yelled. "Bring me a sheet." She hastily grabbed a thin cloth from the pallet closest to her and tied it in a knot to the cargo net separating the trunks and barrels and bags from the sleeping room.

Patience stumbled over with another sheet, and Anna-Marie tied the ends together. She then ran and tied the other end to a post in the center of the room.

Anna-Marie whistled. "Everyone, listen! Get everyone together here. We're going to hold fast to this line and brace ourselves. The airship may be going into a crash. All of the girls who are well, help move those who are sick."

Girls scrambled, slipped, crawled, and even screamed in terror, but Anna-Marie barked orders that would have made a general in any army proud. Everyone in the room held or clutched fearfully at the makeshift tether. Older girls locked elbows with younger girls, none a moment too soon.

The airship careened into the ground with a bone-jarring impact. A few girls lost their grip and slammed into the wall, but most held on. Cargo toppled over and slid or flew through the air. Anna-Marie tightened her grip on the smallest child and leaned away from the cargo net, hoping it was strong enough to stop all of those barrels and crates from breaking through and crushing them.

After rocking a few more times, the airship listed abruptly to the right and came to a shuddering halt.

Anna-Marie exhaled in relief after a moment of stillness. "Everyone okay?" She didn't count the bumps and bruises, the tears and whimpering not bothering her in the least.

All of the girls were safe, awake, and able to answer.

"Sit down and slide to the steps." She let go of the rope and sat on her bottom, scooting the small girl in her arms with her down the now-sloped floor until they reached the stairs to the main deck.

"Can't we stay here?" Celia called, not loosening her grip on the sheet a fraction.

"No. Things may be steady for now, but we don't know if the airship will stay this way."

They didn't know what damage had been caused to the engines sending the lifting gas into the balloon, or if they were at risk for fire. They didn't know if any of the crew, or even the captain, was onboard or if they'd fallen over during the plunge out of the sky. But she didn't give voice to all these dark thoughts. One thing at a time for the girls. They needed calm and order, not chaos and fear. One step in front of the other, and they would get out of this thing.

"I'm going to go up and make sure there is a safe way off," Anna-Marie whispered to Patience, Prudence, and Vivien. "Have the girls ready to move as soon as I return." She split them into groups, each in charge of several girls.

Vivien, wan and pale from her sickness, couldn't hide the fear in her eyes as she gave a tiny nod without argument.

Anna-Marie collected her umbrella from where it had flown from her grasp during the airship's initial drop. Steeling herself for anything, she navigated the sideways staircase with caution but determination. She drew a deep breath before pushing the door. The door refused to budge, but Anna-Marie wasn't surprised. Everything on the ship had to have shifted. She gave it three solid kicks before enough room was carved out to squeeze herself through.

When it crashed into the earth, the ship had settled predominantly on one side. Anna-Marie knew that. She had felt and witnessed it inside, traversed the stairs by crawling along the edges where they met the wall. Yet, somehow, she hadn't prepared herself for the prospect of crossing the deck when it was practically vertical instead of horizontal. Using her arms, she pulled herself out of the hole and around the door.

If the lopsided deck had been daunting, landing on the body that had evidently been the cause of the blocked door was unnerving. Her pulse ticked up, and her breath hitched. She forced herself to roll over the man wearing tan breeches and a loose white shirt. The grizzled face of an older man came into view, and she unclenched the muscles in her jaw.

Not Captain Banks.

Good.

She needed the captain. And she had to make him see reason where the orphan house was concerned. That was all. A perfectly normal reason to be sick at the thought of finding a basic stranger dead.

And really, wouldn't any decent human being care about finding a dead body?

It didn't mean she was being emotional.

Only normal. Practical.

Cold drops of rain pelted her head and neck. She needed to get moving, needed to assess the situation. Near the rear of the ship, the once buoyant balloon now lay fully collapsed, not a breath of air left in it apparently. That would explain the crash.

Though resting on its side, the airship was at least angled in a way that she didn't fall straight into oblivion when she stepped out. Still, the deck was going to be more of a climb then a walk.

Anna-Marie clamored across the deck, using knotholes and cracks between boards to hang on as her legs dangled and toes of her boots scrabbled for purchase. Every time her shoulder ached or stitches burned, she huffed out a breath and pushed thoughts of it aside. After a few feet, she paused to slide her umbrella into a holster on the back of her corset, exactly for a time like this. Well, not necessarily a time when she tried not to fall to her death from a crashed airship that was slick as pig's fat, exactly, but for a time when carrying the umbrella was inconvenient or impossible.

Movement came from near the middle of the deck. It was difficult enough to discern through the rain, but thankfully, the evening was still light enough to see. A crewman bear-walked over a beam to reach a rope. From there, he swung himself down and out of sight. Anna-Marie listened closely. A soft thud sounded, and she assumed the man had safely reached the ground. Voices below confirmed it. She vaguely heard the words "Aye Captain," and relief bloomed in her chest.

She crawled and climbed faster. If she could reach the beam, she might be able to get in speaking range of the men on the ground. She didn't want to yell and alarm the girls below.

Resting her knees on the beam, she began the precarious crawl to the rope dangling farther out. She'd nearly reached it when a hand appeared. Then another. Hand over hand, Captain Banks came into view. Rain dripped from his brow, but his mouth broadened into a wide smile when he noticed her.

"Anna-Marie!" He swung one leg over the beam, then hoisted himself up. "Are you hurt? I was coming back to get you and the girls."

"I'm fine. A few of the girls are banged up, but nothing serious."

"What a miracle!"

Anna-Marie preferred to think of it as an excellent bit of precaution and fast acting, but she wouldn't dally on a beam to discuss the difference. "The girls are scared, and the deck might be difficult for them, but I think we need to get out before anything else happens."

"On it." Banks whistled.

In seconds, a lanky crewman with a shock of orange hair and a completely mechanical right arm came swinging up the rope, easy as pie. He listened as Captain Banks gave him instructions, then scampered around them and down the beam to the deck like a monkey.

"Clancy spends most of his time climbing around the ship to make repairs. He'll get something rigged up in no time. Do you want to get down?" Captain Banks leaned back and tugged the rope forward so Anna-Marie could reach it, but she shook her head.

"I need to get back to the girls." She expected Captain Banks to argue and was pleasantly surprised when he simply nodded and gestured for her to lead the way. Thankful the beam they traversed was thick and wide, she crawled back the way she had come.

She wanted to ask what had happened to make them crash. Was it the storm? If things had gotten worse, should they have landed? Was it because Banks was inexperienced? Or had something more sinister been to blame? Visions of the warehouse exploding came to mind, Cyrus's note that Jack of All Traders was still out there. Had retribution caught up to them? Anna-Marie swallowed every question for now. Safety first. Questions later.

Hammering noises snapped her attention back from her thoughts to the scene around her. Clancy pulled a large wooden shim from a bag at his waist. With one hard strike from his metal fist, he hammered it in place between two deck boards. He continued the process until shims were staggered between the beam and the door to the lower deck. Clancy had created the equivalent of stepping stones. It would still be dicey getting the little girls to balance their way across. but Anna-Marie had to admit it was infinitely better than scrambling along using toe and footholds as she followed the path of shims over to Clancy on the other side of the deck.

Captain Banks was just behind her. Anna-Marie heard a sharp intake of breath and belatedly realized she hadn't warned him about the body. She didn't stop to see how or where he and Clancy moved the crewman to. Anna-Marie clamored inside and down the lopsided staircase, calling out as she went.

"Girls, I'm back. Is everyone ready for an adventure?"

A resounding chorus of no's and maybe one yes made Anna-Marie stifle a laugh. She reached the bottom step and swept her eyes quickly over the group. Two of the smaller girls had fallen asleep, but everyone seemed to be accounted for.

The airship shifted, only an inch or so this time, but it was an excellent reminder that time was of the essence. Captain Banks must have thought the same things because he was suddenly behind her.

"Does Clancy have any more shims?" she asked him softly. At his nod, she said, "We probably need to make the gaps between as small as possible." Her gaze raked over the short legs of some of the girls, and Banks understood.

"I'll be back in a moment." He hurried up the wonky steps. True to his word, he returned in no time, adding shims to shrink the gaps between steps as he came.

Anna-Marie clapped her hands. "Listen up, girls. We have a bit of a tricky trek ahead to get off of this ship. We will *not* be taking any luggage." Her eyes flashed to Viven as she paused to let that sink in. "Everyone, line up. Big girls, spread out between the little ones and offer whatever help you can."

Captain Banks stepped around her and hoisted one of the sleeping forms onto his shoulder. "If you can carry the other one up,

Clancy should be around to take her across and down the rope."

Anna-Marie nodded. She took the little one—tougher than Captain Banks made it look, with arms and legs dangling as dead weight as the girl snored on. Anna-Marie grunted. She'd seen hard sleepers, but this was ridiculous. Struggling up the steps, she was relieved to see Clancy on the first makeshift shim stepping stone. She held up the girl, and he took her in his normal arm without question. He bounced on the balls of his feet across the wooden shims like it was nothing.

Temperance emerged from the door, followed by Captain Banks. The other girls pressed closely behind until Anna-Marie waved a hand to stop them before they pushed each other out.

"Now, like I was saying, this part is going to be tricky."

"Fun," Banks spoke over her last word. "Have any of you ever been to the circus? Or seen the posters? Well, you're about to get to perform a fantastic balancing act of your own. A hop and a skip over these wooden steps will lead you to an awesome rope swing off the ship. Who's ready?"

Prudence nudged Temperance aside. "I'll go."

Anna-Marie watched as Prudence drew a deep breath, then stretched her arms out to the side so one touched the leaning deck and one stretched into the air for balance. Anna-Marie waited until there were two steps between Prudence and the door before helping Temperance up to begin the walk. They continued this way in a tense silence. The rain had lessened to no more than a faint trickle, and Anna-Marie was grateful.

Rosie chewed on her lip as she concentrated. After the first few steps, she laughed. "I'm doing it!"

The last girl in line shook her head and burst into tears when her turn came.

Anna-Marie knelt. "What's your name?"

"Leah."

"Well, Leah. I'm a little nervous. Do you think you could hold my hand and help me across?"

The girl sniffled. Anna-Marie stretched out her palm, and Leah grabbed it. Her tiny, dirty fingernails dug into Anna-Marie's skin as she clutched tighter, but she stepped out onto the shims after Anna-Marie. Clinging tightly, they made slow progress. One of Leah's feet slipped, but Anna-Marie held on to her until she had her balance again.

"Leah, what's your favorite food?"

"Uh, meat pies. I think they're my favorite, though I've only had one."

Anna-Marie smiled as they took the next step. "When we get to Uncle Ernest's, I'll make sure you get all the meat pies you can eat. In fact, we can find someone to teach you how to make them. What do you think?"

"Really?"

"Cross my heart."

Leah smiled through the last trickling tears. "Okay."

They made it to the beam at last, and Anna-Marie heaved a sigh of relief. When Clancy had swung Leah down the rope with the rest of the girls, it was her turn.

"Do you need help?" Captain Banks waited at the end of the beam, offering a hand.

"No, thank you." Anna-Marie pulled her long leather gloves from a pocket, glad she always kept them on her person and not in the carpet bag that was now in the cargo hold for an unforeseeable amount of time. She slid them on her hands and grabbed hold of the rope. Muscles screamed in protest, but she pretended everything was fine as she wrapped her feet around the rope and slid down. The sound of a soft chuckle from Captain Banks made her glance upward, and his twinkling blue eyes met her steel gray ones. He looked impressed and approving, and for reasons she wouldn't examine, that one expression chased away her chill from the rain.

Anna-Marie dropped to the ground more heavily than she normally would have. A prickling sensation in her shoulder told her she'd probably opened at least a few stitches. Banks let go of the rope a few feet from the ground and landed soft as a cat. She acted as if she hadn't noticed.

"Attention!" Captain Banks called.

Anna-Marie watched as the crew assembled into a line. It was easy to see several gaps in it. From the sag of Captain Banks's mouth, she concluded those gaps were men who weren't with them now. Huddled together, the girls drew closer to Anna-Marie. She patted shoulders and hair as several threw their arms around her.

She quieted them and began to check wounds. With a clean corner of her skirt, she wiped a few of the larger scrapes clean but was relieved anew that none of the girls had sustained any serious injuries.

As she worked, she listened to the orders the captain gave his crew. When they began to discuss how to right the airship, she stood up.

"Look where we are now," Vivien snapped. "The middle of nowhere with no way home and no way to this reclusive uncle of yours."

"There's always a way, Vivien."

"How? How do we get anywhere now that our airship is a hulking, ugly landmark."

"Walking. You have feet, just like the rest of us. Now, if you'll excuse me, you and Patience and Prudence can help the girls find a little corner of the field to relieve themselves while I speak with the captain."

Vivien glared. "Do I look like a nanny?"

Anna-Marie rounded on her and hissed, "You look like a spoiled brat who is quite recovered from her illness and is equally stranded as the rest of us. So, try instead to look like a young lady with some decency and help these girls." With that, she stomped away before she said anything to make matters worse. Anna-Marie blamed tea being interrupted for her own short temper.

"Captain Banks? I couldn't help but overhear the dilemma with getting the ship upright to repair it."

"Yes, but we'll get you to Frinton-on-Sea. Don't worry."

"Well, actually, I might be able to help." Anna-Marie pulled him aside. "It's getting harder to see for sure, but I think I recognize that large oak on the hill."

The captain cocked his head to the side as if trying to determine if she was serious. "You believe you recognize a large tree after falling from the sky and landing in a random field somewhere between London and Frinton-on-Sea in the waning amount of evening sunlight we have occasionally peeking through the rain and clouds?" He looped her arm through his elbow. "Perhaps we should sit down, have a look at that head wound."

Anna-Marie shoved his arm away. "I'm quite serious, as well as lucid, thank you. There used to be some mine shafts around the area. I spent a large portion of time exploring them." Training in them, but she wouldn't mention that. "If we make it to the tree and I'm right, there is a tunnel beneath with tracks and carts that could take us within miles of Frinton-on-Sea. Because the tunnels are straighter than the coastline, I'd bet we can make it by morning."

"Hmmm." Banks rubbed his chin. "I like a good bet. It's how I won the *Infamous Inheritance*, did you know? Had to rename her, of course. Wouldn't be caught dead in a vessel called Angry Gryphon. Tell me, mysterious Anna-Marie, what would you be willing to bet?"

"Three pounds?"

Captain Banks shook his head. "Boring. Weren't you listening? I won an airship."

Anna-Marie bristled. "I assure you, sir, that I do not bet with my person if that is what you have in mind."

The captain reared back as if slapped. "I do not take from a lady anything not freely given. When you kiss me, Anna-Marie, it will be because you've fallen for my debonair good looks and irresistible charm, not because I've won a bet."

Anna-Marie could no longer hear the girls or the crew. The hum in her ears was too loud. She didn't even notice the last of the clouds parting and the setting sun blazing bright orange from the horizon. If she had noticed the latter, she would have happily attributed the sudden light as the cause of the warmth creeping up her cheeks.

"*If* I kiss you, not when, it will be to bid farewell to the man who vowed to be looking after my well-being and then nearly sent me plummeting to my death. Before we can part, however, there is the matter of safe delivery of my charges. Therefore, back to the mine."

Captain Banks winked. "If you say so, if you say so. We will walk to this large and utterly familiar oak tree of yours. It will make an excellent camp for the night if there is no shaft or tunnel. If there is not a tunnel, what interesting *item* will you give me for winning the bet?"

Anna-Marie considered. A smile stole slowly across her face. "An umbrella."

"Excuse me?"

"An umbrella. That is my offer if you win. However, *when* you lose, you have to buy a pirate hat." Anna-Marie extended her hand. "Deal?"

"Deal." Banks clasped her hand, but rather than shaking, he turned it and brushed a kiss across her knuckles. Then, he waltzed away without a backward glance, calling for the men to gather any supplies they'd scavenged and any of the girls too tired to walk and make way to the large oak tree on the far hill.

And if the sight of tiny little Leah riding piggyback and giggling as Captain Banks galloped in an absurd manner made her heart open another crack, well, Anna-Marie wouldn't acknowledge that either.

She would close it back up later when she stood on the steps of Uncle Ernest's manor and Captain Banks literally flew away into the great blue yonder, reminding herself the only person you can count on is yourself.

Chapter Sixteen

"Of course, there's a tunnel." Contrary to his tone, Captain Banks didn't look the least bit put out to have lost the bet.

Anna-Marie gave a brief nod. "Of course. I said there would be. By the way, I think your pirate hat should be brown. It will match your breeches and goggles best."

"Brown it is, m'lady. Must maintain my debonair status, even as a pirate."

Anna-Marie kicked herself for not making funding for the orphan house part of the bet, but the thought of those dimples and light hair under a pirate hat was too amusing to pass up. Besides, she wanted to convince him to fund the orphan house because it was the right thing to do, because the responsibility fell to him now that his father was deceased.

"We'll rest for a quarter of an hour and then start into the tunnels." Banks dipped his head to her before making his way between the men. He clapped them on the back, shook hands, conferred quietly.

Soon, coats were spread on the wet grass to create picnic areas. Anna-Marie settled the girls around several while Banks and his men distributed hard cheese, smoked meat, and soggy bread.

Anna-Marie thanked them. as did most of the girls. There wasn't one complaint, unless you counted Vivien, which by this point Anna-Marie did not. The girl would probably complain of the color if she were lying on silk sheets and soft pillows.

Their repast ended far too soon.

"Do we have to go down there?" Temperance leaned around Anna-Marie, staring into the mouth of the mine.

"It is the quickest way."

Celia gulped. "But it's so dark."

Anna-Marie couldn't argue with that one bit. It was one of the reasons Uncle Ernest sent his top tier girls into the tunnels for combat training. It honed all the other senses with such low visibility. She remembered capturing glowworms and setting them loose in the tunnels so there would be a smidgeon of light.

Captain Banks fiddled with something behind them. Several of the girls were already in awe of the dashing captain. They scooted closer.

"What's that?" Patience asked.

Anna-Marie found herself moving closer as well. Banks pulled a large blocky object from a leather pouch. A man next to him—Thatcher, if she recalled—handed him a cylindrical metal object with a wide glass at one end. She smiled. A torch.

"A battery. Once I insert this battery here, and connect these wires there..." He slid a button up on the side, and light spilled from the glass end of the torch.

The girls clapped and gasped in surprise. He had one more and, with both torches blazing, nodded that they could begin.

So, the journey through the tunnels wouldn't be in the pitch black she remembered. Anna-Marie's steps lightened as she led the way into the mouth of the old mine. A few steps brought them to a rudimentary cage lift. Unlike the fancy steam-powered one at the air docks, this one was far older and operated on a pulley system. Someone needed to stay at the top and lower the lift using the hand crank.

Clancy volunteered.

It took three trips to fit everyone down the cage lift to the tunnel. If the girls weren't so thin and small, it would have taken more, though it helped that the original mines had brought small ponies down in the lift to haul coal carts. Clancy swung himself down the lift cable with his metal arm, and the group moved slowly forward.

Mice skittered away from the light. Smells of damp earth invaded their nostrils, but it wasn't an unpleasant scent, as smells go. Spiders crawled up their webs and down the walls on both sides of the tunnel. Anna-Marie bent and picked up a splintered piece of wood to knock webs out of the way. She was petite enough to walk without her head brushing the low dirt ceiling. Most of the men, including Captain Banks, would have to stoop at least an inch or two. The width of the tunnel was about that of two adults, or three of the smaller children.

"Here are the carts." She waved for Captain Banks and Clancy to follow her to several narrow alcoves cut into the wall next to each other. "Can you help me get them on the track?"

Clancy and Thatcher each took an end of a cart, pulling them out. A fat, black snake uncoiled and slithered into the tunnel when his resting place beneath the cart was disturbed, and Anna-Marie screamed.

She couldn't help it. Anna-Marie was completely terrified of snakes. They had always been the worst part of these blasted tunnels.

She ducked behind Banks. "Don't just stand there. Kill it!"

"A woman who can still give orders when she's scared…Great." He pulled a cutlass from the scabbard at his side. Pushing the torch into Anna-Marie's hand and shoving her further away, he swung and smoothly severed the head from the wriggling creature. Not that decapitation ceased the wriggling.

Anna-Marie closed her eyes. It was one of the things she hated about the wily little devils—snakes didn't have the decency to just die and be still.

"Anna-Marie, I didn't know you were scared of snakes," Temperance said loudly.

Vivien rolled her eyes. "I guess Miss Practically Perfect isn't so perfect after all."

"I never claimed to be perfect." Anna-Marie straightened her hat. "I do, however, consider myself perfectly practical, so, snakes or no snakes, we need to get a move on. Snip-snap, let's go, girls. Into the carts."

They piled all of the youngest children into three carts. Anna-Marie had to convince Temperance to ride in the cart instead of sitting on the back with Prudence and Patience to wind the crank that powered set the gears beneath the cart in motion, but the moment the girl settled against the corner and Captain Banks pushed the rumbling cart down the tracks, her eyelids drooped, and her head lolled to the side as she fell fast asleep with the others.

Anna-Marie joined Banks on the first cart and carried the torch. Once the crank was wound, the gears themselves created the perpetual motion required to keep the cart in motion. It was an older form of transportation, placed in the mine long before steam power had captured the hearts and minds of inventors across the country. Occasionally, especially in the case of a sharp turn or steep hill, the crank needed to be turned again to avoid losing much speed.

Prudence and Patience sat together on the platform of the second cart, carrying the second torch. Vivien insisted she needed an escort through the tunnels because she was too weak from the air sickness to continue unassisted as she would certainly faint, fall off, and be run over by another cart. Nothing dramatic, of course.

Anna-Marie rolled her eyes and watched the men drawing straws to determine which of them had to ride through the damp tunnel with Vivien attached to their arm. Thatcher scowled when he lost. Anna-Marie coughed to hide a snicker.

In the lead beside Captain Banks, she pointed the torch straight in front of them, wary of obstacles. The carts rumbling and bouncing along drowned out the noise of any rodents, at least. Every so often, small puddles of water had collected, but they were never very deep. When they'd traveled for some time and she was confident it was too loud to be overheard by any of the girls who were still awake, she asked the question that had been plaguing her.

"Why did the *Infamous Inheritance* go down?"

"It was the storm." Captain Banks sighed.

From the corner of her eye, she could see the corners of his ever-smiling mouth turn down. He ducked his head to wipe sweat from his temple onto his shoulder.

"I knew we weren't near any docking towers yet. I had already asked Admiral Crow—that's what we call the man in the nest who serves as lookout and weather heralder—to find us a reasonable place to take her down in the ocean." He shook his head. "Lightning struck the rudder out of nowhere, closer than any flashes had been before. Wood and metal burnt, and what didn't burst into flame fragmented, shooting shrapnel. One piece pierced the balloon. We couldn't keep enough air in it to stay airborne."

Anna-Marie could tell he blamed himself. And with his status as a completely novice pilot, she wasn't sure that he shouldn't. Before she could think of what to say, a gruff voice from behind them spoke quietly.

"But the captain, he pushed the engine to its limits to keep enough air going in to counteract the air going out," Clancy said. "It was just enough to slow our descent to a rapid fall rather than an instant plummet. We might not have lived, otherwise."

Silence fell again. Captain Banks didn't deny it, but he didn't boast about it, nor did he look any more pleased with himself. Anna-Marie found herself understanding the respectfulness she saw the men display toward him more and more.

They stopped three more times. Twice for water, which the men had thankfully collected in canteens during the rain before the ship crashed. Once for another snake. This time, it was Clancy who saved the day, though Anna-Marie wasn't sure she would ever get the image of him stomping it to death out of her mind. That footwork had been worthy of the best Irish step dancing she'd ever seen. It was just unexpected enough to surprise her, though her skin still crawled with goosebumps, and comical enough that she managed to squeak out mild surprise instead of another scream.

"Are we there yet?" Vivien's whine reached Anna-Marie's ears for the fourth time.

"For the love of tea and biscuits! Yes, we are there."

"Really?"

Anna-Marie rolled her eyes, barely containing the urge to march back there and shake the girl. She was behaving worse than the youngest children. "No, Vivien. The crumbling walls and metal tracks upon which your cart still rolls should be enough to tell you we are, in fact, not there yet without me having to tell you."

"Uh!"

The rest of the dark, damp journey resumed in silence.

Without the torch, Anna-Marie would have been hard pressed to tell when they'd reached the mine's exit. Darkness had fallen outside. Not a hint of light reached the tunnel floor from outside. When the beam of light from the torch in her hand reflected off of the brass and wood cage lift several feet away, Anna-Marie relaxed her grip. Lines and circles indented her palm from holding so tightly to the light for the last hour, hoping the tunnel exit would still be intact.

"We've made it," she called.

Cheers went up from the men. Girls stirred sleepily in the carts, yawning and stretching.

Vivien, of course, couldn't resist a loud and grumpy, "It's about time."

Girls jostled and pushed to be first inside the lift. Everyone wanted out of the tunnel. Though Anna-Marie had overcome her claustrophobia of the place long ago, she, too, ached for fresh air and open spaces, if for no other reason than to disperse the memories.

She gave the torch back to the captain once everyone was safely up and outside again.

Captain Banks stretched and surveyed the landscape with the beam. "What have we here? Another oak?"

"Twin Oak Mines," Anna-Marie supplied.

"How very original," he said dryly. "What adventure do you have in store for us next, mysterious Anna-Marie?"

He said it with such delight, she couldn't even begrudge him the nickname. "I thought about mixing things up, but everyone had so much fun the last few hours that we'll just keep going on a nice long walk."

"I'm tired!"

"I cannot be expected to walk without proper food and sleep."

"Are we there yet?"

"How long?"

The girls piped up all around them. The men, better conditioned to hard work and following orders, nodded, but Anna-Marie noticed the tell-tale signs of exhaustion in those within the circle of torchlight—scrubbing their hands over their faces, long slow blinks.

She sighed. "I suppose everyone wants to rest, then?" Truth be told, her shoulder felt like it had been set ablaze, she was thirsty, and she would love nothing more than to pop open her umbrella and glide the rest of the way to Foxhold Manor in Frinton-on-Sea.

The chorus of hoorays spoke for everyone.

Coats were laid on the ground again. The girls piled on.

Banks and his men organized a night watch schedule. The men who were sleeping first spread out, deliberately sleeping so they created a perimeter circle around the girls and young women. Anna-Marie was grateful but still not comfortable enough trusting in others to go to sleep herself.

A fact Captain Banks clearly noticed.

"You should get some rest too." He rested both of his hands on her shoulders.

She couldn't stop the hiss of pain from escaping between her lips.

"Your shoulder?" he asked.

Anna-Marie feigned nonchalance. "It's fine. Don't trouble yourself over it."

Banks crossed his arms. "You should let me look at it."

Not wanting to wake the girls, or the men, Anna-Marie stepped away from the group. She moved to the oak tree, settling herself on some of the larger exposed roots. "And what could you do about my wound, exactly? It's the middle of the night. We've no medicine, no reason to waste precious drinking water to clean it, and no fresh clothes. Leave it for now. I'll try terribly hard not to take ill and die, costing you the *Infamous Inheritance*, Captain Banks. Besides, I have a reason to be whole and healthy when this journey is ended."

"I've changed my mind."

Anna-Marie narrowed her gaze. "About keeping me alive, or about playing nursemaid?" Her hand instinctively curled around a nearby rock as she forced her posture to remain relaxed.

"Neither." His voice dropped an octave as he leaned in. "I told you to call me whatever you pleased, but I've changed my mind. I'd prefer if you call me Ambrose."

Anna-Marie's throat tightened even as her grip on the rock loosened. She was spared from finding a response when Captain Banks…Ambrose…spoke again.

"You said you had a good reason to be healthy when this journey is over. Pray tell."

Anna-Marie gave the answer she'd had in mind all along. "To see you in a pirate's hat, of course." Rather than relieving the tension, it ratcheted it up more.

A soft, small voice jarred her back to the present. "Anna-Marie?"

"Yes, girls?" she asked Rosie and Celia.

"Can we sit by you?"

"Of course." Anna-Marie patted the tree trunk next to her.

Celia slid down to lean against it. She linked one tiny arm through Anna-Marie's. "The stars are pretty."

"They are." Anna-Marie looked up. The night sky sparkled.

Celia's head fell against her arm, and she gave a rueful smile at how quickly the girls fell asleep. She was surprised to see that Rosie had curled up on the other side of Celia, but her head lay in Ambrose's lap, her eyes closed.

For one brief second, he met her gaze, looking frightened as a startled deer. Then, he shrugged with that casual grace of his, brushed a strand of hair away from Rosie's mouth, and settled against the tree to let the little girl sleep as long as she would.

Chapter Seventeen

Foxhold Manor.

Frinton-on-Sea did not yet rank as a large trading port, though some in the small farming community had big aspirations. Foxhold Manor stood nestled in the midst of carefully landscaped Juneberry trees, paperbark maple trees, and clusters of Mahonia, a sturdy evergreen shrub.

A beautiful prison.

The typical asymmetrical design of large, important houses was a contrast to the symmetrical gardens and walkways in front of the manor. An octagonal turret on the left drew the eye, sweeping one's gaze up to the many-gabled roof. Brown brick with wide, red-brick trimmed windows. Balconies jutted from three of the gables on the second story. Only one room, one tower, encompassed the third floor, and it boasted a clock, ornate as it was massive, that ticked off the minutes and hours with hands designed to look like a key and quill.

Information is the key to all things.

Uncle Ernest's motto.

Anna-Marie slowly rolled her head and neck as they walked down the drive. The girls had laughed and run and picked flowers on the walk across meadows and sheep paddocks, but now their destination was near, they quieted. Nervous whispers flitted across the groups. They walked in huddles, straggling far behind Anna-Marie and Ambrose, unsure of what they would find in yet another new place, but certain it meant their freedom of the past day would be stripped away again.

The crew had agreed to visit the market street by the wharf to buy food and materials to repair the balloon. Ambrose insisted on escorting Anna-Marie and the girls the considerable distance inland to the house. Especially when Anna-Marie explained Uncle Ernest had automatons that functioned as extension scaffolding, which she believed could assist in tilting the airship upright. If they could convince Uncle Ernest to let Ambrose use them...

"I didn't want to bring the girls here." She didn't know why she was telling him this, feet away from the steps to the large porch with the painted-iron hand railings. "I had hoped to have time to come up with an alternative solution."

"Oh? What was your plan?"

She watched him from the corner of her eye as she spoke. "My original plan was to blackmail or shame Lucifer Banks into providing the monetary support he claimed to be providing to the orphan house he was the founder of so the girls would have a decent home and actual meals. To convince him to fire the worthless, drunken overseer and install someone with morals, or at least sense, to run things. I didn't know he was dead." She forged ahead, even though Ambrose's face had gone slack, and they had slowed their steps to a snail's pace. "When that fell through, I bargained with The Procurer to arrange a meeting with Banks's heir and passage out of London, if needed. I didn't know the two would be one and the same," she said with humor. "I was going to convince the heir to step up and do right with his inheritance. Once I met the man, shirking his responsibilities, his title, and his reputation, I determined that ship had also sailed, as it were." Her lips twisted wryly.

"Anna-Marie." Ambrose touched her arm.

"He won't be happy you're here." She changed the subject, stepping up to the large door. Her fingers grasped the knocker.

"I don't care."

"Me neither." She straightened and rapped out five strong knocks.

The door swung open on silent hinges to reveal a staid young parlor maid.

"Hello, Flora."

Flora's lips tipped in a smile, then straightened right away. "Anna-Marie. Uncle has missed you. Won't you come in?"

That was a polite warning Uncle Ernest was seriously displeased she had pulled a disappearing act.

Anna-Marie nodded. It wasn't a surprise. She hadn't planned to come back, after all. "Can you make my guests comfortable in the kitchen while I see him?"

"Of course." Flora bobbed a perfect curtsy. "He's in the workshop."

"Captain Banks, I'll send for you when Uncle Ernest has a proposition for your problem." Anna-Marie injected every bit of formality she could into the statement. The walls had ears. She would not present Uncle Ernest with new leverage over her. Anna-Marie walked away without glancing back.

She strode the familiar path to the heart of the house and the grand stairway. Rather than ascending the steps, she walked beneath them and pulled down on a wall sconce. A panel slid open, silent like so much in this place. A platform with iron railings waited. The panel slid shut behind her as she stepped onto the platform. Triggered by her weight, it moved straight upward. This was the only entrance to the workshop—the only entrance to the third floor at all.

While numerous eccentric tinkerers or scientists had underground workshops, or a wing of rooms set aside, Uncle Ernest built his into the clock tower at the top of the house. Stepping off the platform, she ducked beneath numerous pipes and glanced around. Nothing had changed.

One long wooden table ran along the far wall with various metal gadgets in different stages of creation. Most of those were hers. Uncle Ernest had honed her tinkering abilities, tasking her with creating smaller and smaller listening devices. It was also where she modified her umbrella to harness the flying power of air balloons on a smaller scale. At the end of the table sat a hideous carpet bag, which she had been working on installing a false bottom into that opened and shut by touch of a button. Two more umbrellas hung on the wall between her tools, and she made a note not to leave without them this time. One was a bright yellow parasol. While it didn't fly, it's handle concealed a rapier that had discouraged unwanted advances on more than one occasion. The black umbrella was even deadlier. The tip shot poisoned darts. One scratch was enough to paralyze a grown man for an hour.

The center of the room was taken up mostly by the ladder, platforms, and clockwork mechanisms of the massive clock just above their heads. And yes, it ticked. Loudly.

To the left were shelves of books. Books on mechanics, engineering, physics, alchemy, even herbology. Bookmarks stuck out of many of them, and the edges of the leather covers were faded from use. Next to the bookshelves were assorted bins labeled as cogs, sprockets, gears, pipes, gaskets, and a plethora of other things.

And to the right, a long rack that could lift or suspend things. Uncle Ernest worked with the larger inventions, preferred to move them around for better access rather than to strain himself getting at hard-to-reach places.

"Anna-Marie! Welcome home."

"It's good to be here," she lied with a perfect smile.

Uncle Ernest laughed through his teeth, fizzing and hissing like snakes. It was likely another reason Anna-Marie loathed the creatures, as much as she'd learned to loathe that laugh.

It had been welcome, at first. Amusing. Disarming.

Uncle Ernest laughed at everything. He laughed at dinner, at breakfast, at tea, laughed at jokes, pain, and tears. Uncle Ernest amused himself simply by being amused, she'd determined. Anna-Marie had sincerely hoped never to hear that laugh again.

"Come see what I'm working on."

She joined him, careful to keep her toes out of the vicinity of his wheeled chair.

Uncle Ernest's chair was his pride and joy. He'd modified the design of Joseph Merlin's self-propelled chair so he could whoosh around the room at great speed and agility, thanks to steering levers mounted on a small table above his lap and the hydraulic arms rotating the wheels automatically with the push or pull of one lever. The second lever controlled the direction. When she'd left, he had been working on a seat lift, and it was that very feature he demonstrated now.

"You've finished it?"

Uncle Ernest nodded. "All done. Some of my best work. I can reach the clock without dragging myself up that infernal ladder now." He laughed again.

Uncle Ernest was crippled in both legs. A horse and carriage had run over him as a child. His family had been too poor to afford a doctor and had left Ernest in the street to die. Instead, he crawled to the nearest apothecary and told him his mother had been stealing from him for months. In exchange for her address, he demanded medicine for the pain. And so, he'd learned at a young age that information gained you things you needed. And eventually things you wanted. At least, that's the story he told.

"Congratulations." She patted him on the back.

He might be a great many things she despised, but she knew he was also a man of great intelligence. His inventions, which he sold through a broker under a different name, paid for all of the special tutors that came and went, and their silence.

"Now, tell me who you've brought to my house," Uncle Ernest said, lowering the chair seat down again.

Anna-Marie scooted her own stool over and sat. "Thirty-two orphan girls. I liberated them from a fellow who goes by Jack of all Traders. He's the reason there have been so few orphans on the streets." She could at least give him the information she knew he'd been seeking. It might soften him up for the next thing she had to say. And ask. "Captain Banks flew us here, most of the way, on his airship."

"Most of the way?" *Hiss, hiss*, fizz, spittle came the laughter. "What did he do, fly you the rest of the way with wings?"

"Actually, we crashed. That's why I brought him. We walked the rest of the way here." She would deny going through the tunnel fully and completely if needed. "And I told him you had automatons that could assist in righting the ship so that he could fly back to London."

"You volunteered this without asking?"

"I told him if you were willing, there would be a price." She shrugged as if it mattered little to her. "The sooner the captain is airborne, the farther from here and Foxhold Manor he will be."

Uncle Ernest held her gaze, assessing. "And is that what you want? The captain far away?"

"It doesn't matter to me. Strike a deal with him or don't, the choice is yours. I do have a deal of my own to make."

Laughter shook his body. He wheeled closer until their knees nearly touched. "And just what deal is that?"

"I want to leave. For good. And I want to take the girls I brought today with me." Anna-Marie took a deep breath through her nose. "Jack of all Traders shouldn't be a nuisance for much longer. I blew up one of his factories, and The Procurer is on his trail. You'll have more girls to train and to spy for you. I would like the chance to forge a new path with these girls."

"And what would you give in return for this deal of freedom for you and thirty-two assets?"

Anna-Marie said the next words, fully aware they could be her undoing. "Any last job you want from me, I'll make it happen."

"And if I say no?"

"If you say no, you get no more jobs from me. I'll leave. Over and again. You can hunt me, drag me back, re-train me, kill me, whatever you wish, but you'll lose me as an asset either way. At least my way, you get something you want. Make it important."

The legs of her stool scraped across the wooden floor as she stood. Without another word, she stepped onto the platform and descended to the main floor. Hissing, uncontrolled laughter echoed after her.

Tempted though she was to seek out Ambrose and the girls, Anna-Marie knew she needed to maintain her aloof attitude. She went to the next best place. The lake.

Behind the manor, a two-acre lake sprawled between grassy hills, like a sapphire set in a green velvet jeweler's box. It was serene. She knelt at the edge and splashed water on her arms and face. There would be time to freshen up later. Uncle Ernest would doubtless keep her close for a few days before giving her an answer. For now, she allowed the natural beauty around her to wash away the weariness she felt with the world and the way it treated the less fortunate. The mercy of the streets, the mercy of slavers, even the mercy of someone like Uncle Ernest was nothing short of cruel. The first two, you knew your lot in life, at least. You didn't expect change. Working for Uncle Ernest, she had tasted freedom. Anna-Marie had experienced people treating her like a human being, something more than expendable, as she'd slipped into roles as a governess here or a companion there. And every time, it ended with her breaking their trust—lying, stealing, leaving.

She hated it.

Removing her hat, she lay down in the grass and closed her eyes.

Anna-Marie lost track of time as she drifted off. Only the great clock chiming the noon hour brought her out of her doze.

Uncle Ernest missed most meals in favor of working, so it was a surprise to find him seated at the head of the dining table, but to see Ambrose seated on his left was even less expected.

"Ah, Anna-Marie. Good of you to join us." Uncle Ernest laughed as she settled in the chair to his right.

Anna-Marie couldn't help stealing a glance across the table. Ambrose's lips twitched, and she knew he was struggling not to react to the irritating sound.

Uncle Ernest rang a hand bell, and three footmen appeared, bearing the soup course. He might have come from the gutter, but Uncle Ernest would condone only the finest of things now. "Bad storm yesterday, bad storm," he said over his wine.

And thus, dinner continued from one course and inane topic to the next. Salad. Frinton-on-Sea. Fish. Fashion. Entrée. Airship advancements. At last, dessert was brought out on a long tray. Chocolate pastries, lemon tarts, puddings.

"Captain Banks, I will agree to send my personal automatons to assist with your airship."

Uncle Ernest's abrupt switch to serious matters was not an unusual occurrence. Anna-Marie wiped her mouth with the corner of her napkin.

"That's very generous of you." Ambrose inclined his head.

Laughter shook Uncle Ernest's chest. "Generous? Of course not. You'll be repaying me with a favor."

Ambrose raised an eyebrow. "I see. Might I inquire what this favor will be before we are decided? It might be that I can raise the ship on my own."

Anna-Marie placed her hands in her lap so her tension would not show as she squeezed the napkin. She wanted to warn Ambrose to tread carefully, but he wouldn't look at her, and that was likely for the best, anyway.

"You may, but I don't think you'll find this favor a hardship. Good ol' Albert is hosting an inventor's consortium." Laughter punctuated the sentence as he spoke of the prince. "The Great Exhibition, they say, will be a place where great minds gather. I'd like you to take Anna-Marie. She has a great interest in these things, and I can't exactly escort her myself without being noticed.

You, being part of that blessed upper echelon of society, should be able to mingle and blend into a crowd with no great effort. Harder will be obtaining an invitation to a private gathering the queen is holding while the exhibition is taking place."

Ambrose glanced at Anna-Marie, but she kept her face perfectly neutral. She didn't know what Uncle Albert wanted from that exhibition, but she'd bet her hat he wanted something. She would let Ambrose think it was a simple matter of attending a fascinating event. In the grand scheme of things that could have been demanded as payment, this one was relatively harmless, at least for him.

Ever the gentleman, Ambrose extended his hand. "You have a deal."

Chapter Eighteen

The automatons did their job well.

Anna-Marie flipped the switch to open the top hatch and climbed out of the one she'd been operating. By spreading out four of the inventions on one side of the boat, pushing it upward with the rectangular, flat extension platform, while men from the crew pulled on ropes attached to grappling hooks on the other side, they were able to push and pull, push and pull, until the ship was upright again. Two of the automatons had been relocated to the opposite side, and now the four served as a makeshift dock on dry land, stabilizing the ship.

Ambrose itched to oversee the repairs, but he had a debt to pay. Anna-Marie could see how it irked him when Uncle Ernest insisted she and Captain Banks needed to return to London ahead of the *Infamous Inheritance* in order to obtain the coveted invitation, not to mention appropriate clothing to attend. She managed to sneak into the dormitory to tell the girls to enjoy their lessons while she was gone, promising to tear-stained faces she would return for them.

"Uncle Ernest will insist on checking in on your crew with surprise visits. He's a bit paranoid about his automatons being destroyed or stolen." Anna-Marie and Ambrose were in the carriage Uncle Ernest leant them for the ride to the nearest train station. They had been riding for hours. Anna-Marie explained how she had come into the dubious employ of Uncle Ernest what felt like a lifetime ago, but was truly only a couple of years.

Ambrose nodded. "I just hope the men make the repairs quickly. I don't like the thought of my airship being so far away."

They fell into a companionable silence for a few miles. None of the tension from the night before was present, likely because both were so absorbed in their own thoughts. Anna-Marie replayed in her head every detail of the instructions Uncle Ernest had given her, in private, before they departed.

"This is an important job, as I'm sure you've surmised, my girl". Laughter. "I need you to bring me something."

She had remained silent. Guessing only amused Uncle Ernest. He thought himself far smarter than anyone else. Instead of playing games, she simply waited to be told what to steal. She reminded herself this would be the last time.

"You're probably thinking it is one of the inventions that I'm after. You're wrong. Not one of the

inventor's either." Fizz, hiss, hiss, fizz came the spray of laughter between his teeth. "What I want is far, far more important than any single gadget. It could change the world. It isn't part of the exhibition. It is going to be on the person of one of the visiting dignitaries. You will need to be in close proximity when he meets with the queen privately to see the book, to find out where he keeps it. I'm sure, with your significant skills, a musty old book will be no trouble."

Of course, she couldn't resist asking what the book was and why it was so important. This had sent Uncle Ernest into another fit of laughter. He didn't tell her, of course. Only sketched her a picture of the book, told her to memorize it, then took it back and dissolved it in acid.

The carriage clipped along at a fast pace, and Anna-Marie pulled back the curtains. They would be arriving at the station soon. She put the image of the leather book, with the iron lock set with a deep black moonstone in the center, out of her mind.

It was Ambrose who broke the silence next. He cleared his throat. "About the invitation. I didn't want to jeopardize things, so I didn't mention it to your, erm, uncle, but I'm not exactly in with society these days."

"What do you mean?"

"Even before father died, he cut me off. I gambled away the last of my money in self-pity. It was quite fortunate when I won."

"Ah, the *Infamous Inheritance*." The name made much more sense now. "Why were you cut off?"

"I wanted to explore instead of be married off in favor of one of father's political alliances. I hoped to discover things, achieve things, good things."

"Things such as?"

"I'm not sure I knew, exactly. I just knew I didn't want to be like my father. Making promises in front and cutting deals behind, only looking out for himself." Ambrose scowled. "I honestly didn't know about the orphan house. I should have looked into things closer at home rather than trying to run away from it all."

The carriage rolled to a stop. A cacophony of noise assaulted their ears as the footman opened the door: steam releasing from the carriage and a hiss as it cooled down, horses, steam autos, people calling out to one another, the whistle of an arriving train's horn and screech of brakes.

Anna-Marie went in the station and bought two tickets—Uncle Ernest did always send enough money to get the job done, plus some, when he handed down assignments—while Ambrose collected their luggage from the carriage and hailed a porter. She had been relieved to be reunited with her carpet bag from the airship, but for this trip, she'd finished installing the false bottom on the purple-flowered monstrosity of a carpet bag and brought it instead.

"All aboard!"

They handed their tickets to the conductor to punch. Crowds jostled onto the train, the scent of multiple perfumes and colognes tickling Anna-Marie's nose. She rubbed it to avoid a sneeze when an obnoxiously large peacock feather brushed against her face. The woman wearing the offending feather and equally offending hat would have perished on the spot if she'd seen the glare Anna-Marie shot her backside.

It couldn't be denied that excitement was in the air. Children giggled and ran down the aisles until pulled back into seats by scolding mothers. Men bent heads together as they produced newspapers and pointed, talking over one another.

Ambrose nudged her elbow. His breath stirred the hairs at her neck as he bent to whisper in her ear. "It appears we aren't the only ones with an interest in this Great Exhibition."

"Half of England must be going." It wouldn't make a difference to her task, of course. Going unnoticed in such a crowd would certainly be easier, but the crowded consortium wasn't her target. A private meeting in some inner sanctum of the Crystal Palace wouldn't be impacted by such a massive swarm of people, unless it were to up security, making her job harder instead of easier.

Two blasts of the whistle announced the train pulling out of the station. A small lurch caused Anna-Marie to stumble, but Ambrose steadied her with a hand against the small of her back. The slow chug forward soon sped up, and the station grew smaller behind them.

Anna-Marie and Ambrose pressed through the people. When she passed all of the passenger seats, opened a door at the end of the car, and prepared to step across the couplings to the next car, Ambrose practically dove in front to block her path.

"Where exactly are you going?" He glanced pointedly down at the tracks speeding away beneath them.

"To the parlor car, of course." Anna-Marie lifted the owl pocket watch from her corset. "It's nearly time for tea. I will not have my schedule interrupted."

Ambrose waved his arm with an exaggerated bow. "By all means, please, leap to your death for a cup of Earl Grey."

"Oh, for the love of tea and biscuits, are you always so dramatic?" In a move full of grace, Anna-Marie catapulted over the railing and used her momentum landing on the coupling to spring back into the air and onto the adjoining balcony. "Are you coming?"

Ambrose pretended to think about it. The tap of his fingers to his chin drew her eye, and his mouth curved into a teasing grin.

"If you thought to impress me, think again. I'm convinced you're capable of anything already, mysterious Anna-Marie. However, it is you who should prepare to be amazed." Stepping his long legs over the railing, Ambrose turned around and lowered himself down, facing backward, onto the metal bars connecting the rail cars. Placing both hands out to the side, he walked across. Unfortunately, he misjudged the placement of the pin in the coupling. His ankle bumped against it, and his arms pinwheeled as he tried but failed to gain his balance.

Quick as lightning, Anna-Marie snaked her umbrella out and hooked the handle beneath his armpit, jerking him to the balcony in front of her and catching his other shoulder with her free hand.

"If you wanted me in your arms, all you needed to do was ask," Ambrose joked.

"Buffoon." She let go. "I should have let you fall."

Ambrose climbed over the rail onto the balcony beside her. With a tug, he straightened his waistcoat and shirt. "Admit it. You're growing fond of me."

"Almost as fond as I am of snakes," she said dryly. "Let's go before the tea is cold."

Ambrose opened the door. "Ladies first."

The parlor car was opulently appointed with plush oriental carpeting, chandeliers, and ornately carved wood trim around the ten rectangular windows, five on each side. Three large tables were laid elegantly for tea, with fine bone china tea sets at each.

All six chairs at the first table were fully occupied. Anna-Marie barely spared a glance for the three matronly ladies and their tittering charges. The latter were on the way to London to snare husbands, no doubt, or at least that was their hope.

The second table boasted three empty chairs, but Anna-Marie passed it by as well. She had no desire to share a table with a dour-faced old spinster and her equally serious-looking fox terriers. The dogs sat in chairs of their own, resigned, reminding her rather of little old men whose wives nagged far too much.

The last table was occupied by only one person, and even if each of the other tables had been completely empty, she would have been compelled to come sit at this one. Not to mention, it afforded easy access to the rear door of the parlor car. One could never be too careful where strategic exits were concerned, a fact the man at the table appreciated as well as she did.

Ambrose stiffened beside her when he saw her purpose but pulled a chair out at the table for her politely all the same. The chair farthest away from Cyrus, to be specific.

"Cyrus."

"Sweet little Anna-Marie." Her name was a purr on his lips. "Fancy meeting you here, love."

Ambrose sat in the chair on Anna-Marie's right. With a flick of his napkin to his lap, he helped himself to a biscuit. "And I'm Captain Banks. Nice to see you again. Isn't this just cozy."

Cyrus raised an eyebrow.

"Don't feel bad, old chap. I'm sure it is difficult to remember every single solitary person that you threaten, but I'm the captain of the airship you threatened to turn to ash if anything were to happen to Miss Pauper." Ambrose took a large bite, closing his eyes as if it was heavenly. "I won't hold it against you, though. Not everyone is capable of learning good manners."

Anna-Marie didn't know whether to laugh or to groan. The man truly took nothing seriously.

"I suppose you'll both be wanting me to pour, then? If I must, I must." She tipped the kettle to fill each cup in turn.

Cyrus held a hand up to stop her at the halfway mark. He pulled a flask from his boot and tipped it into the cup until the liquid rose to the brim.

"No spoonful of sugar, then?" Anna-Marie quirked a brow.

Cyrus stirred his tea and threw it back in a single gulp. "I've learned a spoonful of anything from you can be dangerous." His eyes twinkled.

"I'll take a spoonful—three, actually." Ambrose served himself from the sugar bowl, then offered it to Anna-Marie. "I admit, I have a sweet tooth. Can't help myself."

Anna-Marie added one sugar, stirred her tea, and sipped. She allowed the familiar ritual to calm her squirming insides. If these two didn't stop their alpha male games, she feared one of them would get up to relieve himself on her leg soon.

Once she collected herself, she got right to the point, as usual. "What are you doing here, Cyrus? Surely you haven't stooped to following clients to retrieve payment yourself? I thought busting people up for cash was beneath The Procurer these days, when you have goons to send."

Cyrus leaned forward, his voice a silken whisper. "Let's be clear. I haven't yet given up on you changing your mind about cash being the form of payment, but no, I am not here because of you. I was following a lead."

Ambrose might have growled something along the lines of "bloody hell," but Anna-Marie ignored him.

"Let's be doubly clear. Here is your cash. My debt is cleared." She reached beneath her wide leather belt to a concealed pocket. Pulling out several pounds, she placed it on Cyrus's folded napkin.

He deftly closed the napkin and pocketed everything. "Disappointing, but not unexpected."

"And your lead…would that happen to be on our mutual acquaintance?" Anna-Marie poured another steaming cup of tea for herself.

Done with pretense, Cyrus took a sip from his flask. "That's right. The man is in the market for new real estate for some unfathomable reason. My sources say that isn't why he came this way. I'm told he's looking for someone."

Anna-Marie frowned. How would Jack of all Traders know who she was, much less which part of the country to look for her in?

Ambrose glanced between the two of them. "Not to intrude, but are you saying the man whose factory Anna-Marie blew up is trying to find her?"

Cyrus's mouth pulled into a thin line.

"Yes," Anna-Marie answered. Goodness, the tension between these two was suffocating. "Cyrus, as Ambrose and I will be traveling together for the next several days—"

"Or weeks. Who knows where fate may take us?"

She glared at Ambrose for baiting the man across from them, but he grinned unrepentantly. If the two thought they were impressing her with all this posturing, they were coming closer to making her swear off men for a lifetime.

"He has a vested interest in things or people surrounding me for the time," she finished speaking. "It's your own fault," she added. "You did link my safety to his airship."

"Ah, yes. The airship." Now it was Cyrus's turn to look like the cat who swallowed the canary. "Where is your pride and joy? Could your incompetence as a captain be the reason today's travel is by train, instead?"

Ambrose didn't even bristle. "Not at all. My incompetence as a lightning rod proved to be our downfall."

Anna-Marie steered the topic back to Jack of All Traders. "Did the lead pan out?"

"No." Cyrus leaned back in his chair with a sigh. "He vanished like smoke. Whoever he is, he either wasn't here, or he's good at blending in. You haven't had any other mishaps besides the weather? No feelings of being watched?"

She thought on the question. Anna-Marie couldn't answer negative to that because Uncle Ernest was always watching, a feeling that had followed her relentlessly the short period of time she'd been back at Foxhold Manor. "Nothing out of the ordinary."

"I've answered your questions. Time for some of my own." Cyrus tilted his head. "Where are you two going, alone, without the band of ragamuffins you seemed so willing to die to rescue?"

"I'll be escorting Anna-Marie to The Great Exhibition. It's a consortium, fancy word for gathering, where people who prefer to use their brains over their brawn gather and pave the way for advancements in technology and improved ways of life." Ambrose answered before Anna-Marie could form a more cautious response.

To The Procurer, all information was currency, and she wasn't sure what he might use theirs for. At least she hadn't shared with Ambrose her true mission at the exhibition.

If Cyrus guessed there was more beneath the surface, he didn't press. "It is fortunate for men without much fortitude for heavy lifting and dirty work to have spectators willing to come watch them parade their metal toys around. Fortunately for society, some of us are blessed with large muscles and equally large brains."

Anna-Marie snorted at the way he paused before the last word. "I do believe I'm going to search out some of those individuals with large brains. I'd be satisfied with medium-sized brains, as a matter of fact, someone with the simple capacity of holding a civil and remotely interesting conversation to pass the time on this infernal train."

She should have simply flown her umbrella. Unfortunately, she was still working out a solution for steering during long distance trips, and Uncle Ernest had insisted she needed to put on a good show of being quite attached to Captain Banks in order to be included on the invitation to the queen's private meeting.

Two sets of footsteps sounded behind her. For the love of tea and biscuits, could the dratted men not take a hint?

Chapter Nineteen

The long ten-second blast from the train whistle and the call of the conductor that they were approaching London's Euston Station was the most beautiful noise Anna-Marie had ever heard.

She felt like years of her life had been stolen. The fact the journey had taken barely over an hour by rail was completely irrelevant. Ambrose and Cyrus had insisted on staying by her side the whole trip. Cyrus insisted that with Jack of All Traders supposedly sniffing after her, his goal of catching the man would be best accomplished by being with Anna-Marie.

She had seen the look in Ambrose's eye that said he was about to blab too much about the exhibition being a favor for Uncle Ernest requiring he be very near, and she had resolutely agreed to having them both close for the foreseeable future. A decision that was far more likely to be the death of her than Jack of All Traders. She would welcome a good life-threatening ambush right now, anything to rid her of the malevolent looks of Cyrus and bemused winks of Ambrose. Anna-Marie had threatened to cut out both of their tongues if they continued speaking to or about her. Who knew they could be just as immature and frustrating while silent?

Anna-Marie accepted the arm offered by Ambrose. He escorted her to claim their luggage, while Cyrus disappeared into the crowd. Anna-Marie knew he hadn't truly gone far. He would watch and follow from a distance, waiting to see if Jack of All Traders revealed himself.

Ambrose flipped a coin to a news boy and collected a paper. He tapped the headline. "It looks as if we have three whole days to prepare for The Great Exhibition. What a nightmare!"

"What is?" Anna-Marie scanned the crowd from beneath the brim of her hat.

"I'm going to have to go see my mother, who probably still hates me and blames me for my father's untimely death. Last I saw her, I believe she cited embarrassment as the cause of his heart attack. On top of that, we have to get something for you to wear that is acceptable for being presented to the queen and in less than a week." Ambrose clucked his tongue. "No tailor could possibly be talented enough to pull it off in such a short time. It's madness."

"Then perhaps madness, not talent, is what we need." Anna-Marie grinned.

Ambrose led Anna-Marie away from the train station, past the automatons at the gate that were supposed to deter pickpocketing. Anna-Marie chuckled as a small boy of six used a stick to knock the whistle from the copper's metal fingers and then ran squealing away, to the cheers and laughs of a gang of boys the same age.

Their walk was not unpleasant. The air was cool but not cold. Anna-Marie did note she would need to get a new overcoat for evenings, as hers had not survived the blast of the cotton factory.

Ambrose stopped in front of a classically wealthy home on Park Lane.

He stood and stared at the door morosely for so long Anna-Marie finally stepped in front of him, hands on her hips. "Well?"

"Well, what?"

"Do you plan to go in, or shall I simply take your bags to your room through the window? We can't cart this luggage down Bond Street and not expect to be beaten and robbed. At least you would be beaten and robbed. I would more likely find myself on yet another gang's retaliation list after having to dispatch your assailants. A most inconvenient way to begin a shopping trip, if ever there was one."

"Can you?"

Anna-Marie's brows furrowed. "Can I what? Dispatch a gang of assailants? Of course."

"No. Can you take the bags in through the window?" Ambrose laughed. "It's perfect. Why didn't I think of it? Here." He grasped her hand and tugged Anna-Marie to the side of the austere home. "It's just there." Ambrose pointed up to a second-story window.

"You are serious, aren't you?" Anna-Marie huffed. She jerked her hand back, unnerved by the way the warmth surged through her while he held it.

"Completely serious."

"Captain Ambrose Banks, you joke about everything in the world, but right now, you honestly want me to scale the side of a house and put your luggage inside so that you don't have to reconcile with your mother?"

"I'm sparing you an introduction to the old dragon at the moment. You should be thanking me." He nudged her into the bushes. "Go on, I'll give you a leg up, shall I?"

She grumbled halfheartedly, but the truth of the situation was, they were short on time, and this seemed to be the quickest course of action. Ignoring Ambrose's interlaced fingers, Anna-Marie opened her carpet bag to remove a length of rope, which she used to bind the two suitcases Ambrose had brought.

She handed the rope to Ambrose. "Be ready to toss me the rope." With a flick of her wrist, she opened her umbrella. A click of a button later and she was rising into the air.

"I guess a fellow could have done worse than winning an umbrella from you in a gamble, then," Ambrose mumbled below.

Anna-Marie caught the windowsill and braced herself. She closed the umbrella and nudged the window open, climbing inside. Once she had assured herself the room was empty, she leaned back out and gestured for the rope to be tossed up.

Once all of the bags were tucked into a closet where they wouldn't attract the attention of any maids who came in to dust, Anna-Marie returned to the ground by sliding down a rain spout.

Feathered hats, ruffled skirts, crushed velvets, bright silks, and intricate cravats all flounced down Bond Street. At least, the people wearing them flounced and strolled and paraded themselves for all to see. It was a practice Anna-Marie detested, having come from a place of nothing. However, one thing was certain—if she wanted to blend in enough to be accepted as one of the elites of society, she would have to join all of these painted peacocks in trying to stand out.

Ambrose extended his arm.

Anna-Marie placed her hand through it, grasping his strong forearm, telling herself it was best to keep up appearances if they were to be a couple at the expedition. She didn't enjoy the feel of the heat spreading from Ambrose's arms up her own. And she didn't like the pretense to be closer to him or feel the urge to smirk at all of the silly, eyelash-batting girls whose lips turned down in pretty pouts when Ambrose didn't glance at them. Not at all.

"I have to ask…" Ambrose interrupted her thoughts. "You've passed the two most popular modistes and at least one fine milliner. Where are we going?"

As they neared the end of the fashionable street, Anna-Marie turned left. Just past the corner, an ornate brass and wood sign hung above a whitewashed door. Two windows showed very little in the dim interior.

"Welcome to Madame the Hatter's." Anna-Marie pushed open the door, inhaling the scents of leather and tea.

"Anna-Marie!" A curvaceous woman with pert lips and outstretched arms dropped the bolt of white lace she'd been wrapping around a mannequin and captured Anna-Marie's face between her hands, planting a kiss on each cheek. "It has been far too long since I have seen you darken my door." Her light French accent gave each of her words a melodic quality.

"Too true, Madame. Allow me to introduce Captain Ambrose Banks." She leaned forward to speak in conspirational tones. "He's in the market for a very special hat."

Ambroses's brows flew to his hairline. "That's why we're here? You simply can't wait a single moment to get me in a pirate's hat, when we need a wardrobe fit to impress a queen?" He gave a longsuffering sigh and turned to Madame. "The things I put up with for this one. She can't sleep, barely eats, all because she wants me to play the part of her fantasy pirate."

Anna-Marie rolled her eyes, and Madame laughed heartily. "It is good you have brought this friend," she said to Anna-Marie. She stared a moment at the pair, then nodded. "Oui. Very good. He is good for you. Makes you alive again. Come, come. I have just the things you need."

"How can she have everything we need when she's taken no measurements?" Ambrose whispered. "Have you forgotten, time is not a luxury we have?"

"Madame always has everything. She lets people believe she has a bit of the sight. Sight, spies, uncanny intuition, whatever it is, she has never disappointed me." Anna-Marie sighed. "Most of London doesn't realize she is here. Those that do think she's mad, but I think she's bloody brilliant."

Madame led them not to a display of hats, but to a small table behind a curtain. The table bore three place settings, a steaming kettle of tea, and a stack of scones next to a pot of clotted cream.

"See. Exactly what we needed." Anna-Marie waved her pocket watch at Ambrose. To Madame she said, "You've outdone yourself."

Over tea and scones, Anna-Marie explained about their need for clothing that would help in their quest of getting noticed and invited to the smaller gathering being held by the queen. She also regaled the woman with the story of Ambrose's ill-fated bet and the reason he now required a pirate's hat.

When they finished their tea, and Ambrose polished off the very last scone, Madame returned to the front of the store, hung a closed sign on the door, and locked it. She then bid them follow her once more.

Anna-Marie knew what came next, so she watched Ambrose's eyes widen as Madame placed a slipper-clad foot on the table between the cream and the sugar and climbed up.

When she started pressing on the wooden ceiling, he stretched his arms out like he didn't know if he should assist her or brace himself in case she fell on him.

"Voila!"

Ambrose looked from the staircase lowering down from the ceiling to Anna-Marie and back. "Interesting place to keep your hats." He straightened his shoulders and followed Madame upward.

By the time Anna-Marie joined them in the hidden room, Madame was lifting dustcovers off of various mannequins. Her lips parted in surprise and awe at the last thing revealed.

"Oh!" She moved at once to touch the gorgeous creation. The dress was frothy and feminine in material but practical and business-like in cut. The black silk skirts interlaced with leather straps and pouches, and the overskirt ruffled above the knees for easy movement. No bustle or hoop, it would allow complete freedom of movement. A bronze leather corset fastened around the middle. Marie lifted her fingers across the sides and front. No boning—perfect.

And the overcoat was nearly identical to the one she'd lost. This one was much shorter, stopping at her waist, but it still had several pockets.

"There are eight more on the inside," Madame said, following her gaze. "You should be able to carry most anything small that needs concealing."

"It is truly lovely, thank you. What do you say, Ambrose? Will this do for an outing at The Great Exhibition?"

Silence met her question. Anna-Marie pulled her gaze from the custom garment and searched out Ambrose. Across the room, he stood in front of a mirror.

Ambrose turned his head left then right as he tried on the hat Madame had shown him to. "Do you think it's too many feathers?"

"Absolutely not!" Anna-Marie joined him at the mirror. "In fact, if I'm not mistaken, you might want one or two more."

"More?" Ambrose's Adam's apple jumped.

"Oh, yes. Madame, would you like to tell dear Captain Banks about these feathers?"

Madame gestured for Ambrose to give her the hat. He did so, eyes narrowed warily between the two women, as if he were trying to determine what manner of joke they were playing on him.

As he watched, Madame selected a long black feather and pulled. His confusion turned quickly to surprise. "A quill. Rather ingenious. Too bad there isn't a pot of ink in there as well."

"It is refilling." Madame gave the hat to Anna-Marie to hold. Quickly, she demonstrated how to remove the metal nib from the feather. "You pour ink into this part"—she indicated the silver tip—"then put them back together. In the hat is a place to stick the quill that will keep ink from spilling."

"Marvelous. Still, there are three feathers, and I doubt I need more quills than that. I'm not a particularly lengthy letter writer."

"It is a good thing each feather is different." Madame replaced the quill and tugged out the next feather. A thin blade glinted from the end.

"Poison dart. Don't scratch yourself with this one." Madame stuck it back in the hat while Ambrose stood, shaking his head.

"And the third one?" he asked.

"That one is just a feather."

Anna-Marie laughed as Ambrose's face fell. "I told you that you would want more feathers," she said. She studied the goggles and compass adorning the hat before handing it back to him.

"Thank you, Madame, for this fine hat." Ambrose put it back on his head. "I do believe it is my favorite one."

"Oui, of course it is," she said in a tone that brooked no argument. "Now, let's get the rest of your wardrobe taken care of so the two of you can be on your way. I have a business to run, you know."

By the time they strolled back onto the street, Madame had promised to have two more dresses and several articles of men's clothing in matching colors delivered to Ambrose's mother's residence the next day. Ambrose insisted on wearing his new hat right away.

"Admit it. You love the hat."

"I do agree that it looks rather more dashing on you than ridiculous. I'll have to do a better job of choosing humiliating stakes next time that we bet." Anna-Marie sighed theatrically.

"Dashing?" Cyrus materialized from behind a post. "I don't think so. More like you've just come from playing dress-up in the schoolroom."

"And here I'd hoped we had parted ways for good." Ambrose frowned. "To what do we owe the displeasure of your company?"

"Jack of All Traders is back in the city." Cyrus touched Anna-Marie's wrist. "My sources say he isn't after orphans anymore. Grown men are going missing from the docks, the streets, even outside of gentlemen's clubs. Whatever he's up to, it seems to be escalating with the crowds in town for the exhibition. Watch your backs."

Cyrus disappeared down a side street.

"That's not ominous," Ambrose mused.

Anna-Marie frowned. "It doesn't really make sense though, does it. Why switch from small children to grown men? He isn't putting them to work in a cotton factory." She didn't like unpredictability. More than that, she didn't like that Jack of All Traders was still out there, no matter what new scheme he was working.

The walk back to Park Lane passed mostly in silence.

They drew even with the steps just as a carriage pulled to a stop out front.

"So much for going in through the window," Ambrose muttered. Then, he pasted on a smile and turned to the woman being handed down. "Mother!"

Anna-Marie took a moment to assess the woman, who evidently struck fear into her grown son. She was petite, smaller even than Anna-Marie herself. While her hair was silver at the edges, nothing about her gave credence to the old dragon image Ambrose had spoken. In fact, she appeared on the verge of fainting at the mere sight of Ambrose standing in front of her, and Anna-Marie thought he must have been teasing her about his mother all along. Until the woman opened her mouth.

"Be still my heart! It's my son, returned to me from the dead," she screeched. "For surely, you must have been dead. There is no other excuse for leaving one's mother to mourn and grieve alone these months. You would never be so callous to an old woman. Therefore, I must go in at once and give thanks for whatever circumstance has given life back to your body and brought your feet in the direction of home at last."

"Mother, you're causing a scene. Can we go inside?" Ambrose gently approached the tiny woman, but she thrust her pocketbook at him.

"No, no! Don't help me now. I'm quite used to escorting myself, alone, anywhere I need to go. I think I'll go lie down. Who knows, perhaps this is all an overtaxing dream? If it is not a dream or hallucination"—she narrowed her eyes at him—"I would expect to see you dressed for dinner in two hours."

With that pronouncement, she swept up the steps and into the house without a backward glance.

"Maybe I should go…"

"Don't you dare leave." Ambrose held his hands up. "Besides, your bag is inside."

"I could just go through the window to get it," Anna-Marie pointed out.

"No. You can't leave me alone with my mother. Besides, if we are to be a couple for this week, you'll have to meet her at some point." Ambrose held out an arm.

With a sigh that was much less reluctant than it should be, she allowed him to escort her inside.

Chapter Twenty

Anna-Marie freshened up in the room Ambrose had made up for her. The powder-blue wallpaper with golden roses was a bit much for her taste, but the rest of the room was nicely appointed.

Dinner turned out to be a formal affair, even for the three of them.

A footman pulled out her chair, and Anna-Marie sat down under the withering gaze of Lady Banks.

"Allow me to introduce my good friend, Anna-Marie. Anna-Marie, my mother, Lady Hester Banks." Ambrose kissed his mother on the cheek before seating himself across from Anna-Marie.

"At least you've decided to settle down and produce heirs."

Ambrose choked on his wine, and Anna-Marie blanched. She looked from Ambrose to his mother. Was the woman talking about her?

Hester breezed ahead. "We will need a few weeks to call the bans. Hopefully, that will be enough time before a babe is evident, and we can invent a proper lineage for your future wife."

"Mother!" Ambrose exclaimed.

"What other reason would you bring a lady friend unannounced into my home and expect me to feed and house her with no notice, my boy?" Lady Banks raised a spoon of soup to her mouth, features neutral as if she were discussing the weather. "I hope she doesn't think she will get her claws into your father's wealth. There will be a marriage contract, of course."

Anna-Marie rose, tossing her napkin on the table. "Pardon me? I assure you that I do not have such a relationship with your son. While I may not be of peerless character like your ladyship, I do have my own standards, and one of them includes not being spoken of as if I'm not in the room. You may rest assured, I do not have designs on your son or your wretched, lying, worthless husband's money, other than to see that his duty to the orphan house in this city is done. Perhaps you believe yourself above me in station, but I can see now you are just the dragon Ambrose described you to be in nature. Good day."

"Really, Mother?" Ambrose sounded tired, but he rose and strode after Anna-Marie.

"I'm leaving."

"So I gathered." Ambrose sighed. "Stay. It would be the perfect way to respond and show her she isn't going to get away with speaking that way.

Plus, you wouldn't be leaving me to her temper when I explain she will not be planning a wedding."

"Good luck." Anna-Marie fumed all the way up the ornate staircase. "I'll see you day after tomorrow."

"Where will you stay? And why not tomorrow?"

"I'll go to the orphan house." Anna-Marie paused in the corridor, picturing the location of the window she'd climbed in only hours ago. Determining which door must belong to that room, she marched off again. "I have reconnaissance to do. I'll come for my clothes in two days and discuss our plan."

"Terribly risky for you to leave me here. She might just lecture me to death, you know." Ambrose tossed up his hands. "Then what would you do, with no escort?"

Anna-Marie's eyes rested on the hat at the foot of his bed. "I'd find myself another pirate, I suppose."

Ambrose laughed. "Don't you know? There's no other pirate like me." He caught her elbow, spun her around. "Won't you stay?"

"I can't. I might strangle that woman, and then you'd be an orphan too," she joked. At least, she thought she was joking. For someone who normally didn't care what people thought, who was used to slights, her blood was certainly boiling at the way Lady Banks had both assumed she was after Ambrose and dismissed her as important all in the same breath. She made it clear Anna-Marie wasn't worthy of her son, and why that should be so bothersome, she didn't want to examine. She needed to escape from this house where she clearly didn't belong.

"You seem to especially like orphans. Maybe it wouldn't be so bad." Ambrose attempted a rakish wink completely at odds with his lopsided grin, holding her gaze.

Anna-Marie looked at him, and her breath caught. Though his words and manner were all joking, his eyes searched hers intently. His smile remained as glib as ever, but he held her as if he were holding a lifeline, and her breath caught. Her lips parted, and his breath hitched. The sound shook her free from whatever this moment was, and she stepped out of his grasp. She wouldn't believe he was serious. Wouldn't believe he wanted her to care for him. His mother was right. He would need a wife and children, would need to fit into this life that she never could. Ambrose was simply in denial of it right now—playing pirate on his airship until he came back home to do his duty.

Anna-Marie cleared the lump in her throat. "I'm sorry I told your mother you thought she was a dragon," she said.

Ambrose ran a hand through his hair. "I was rather hoping she didn't hear that part."

Anna-Marie laughed. "Unlikely."

"I'll straighten everything out. Don't worry about me."

Before she knew what was happening, Ambrose met her at the door and kissed her. A simple, chaste kiss, a whisper across her lips at best.

It was so unexpected, she did something she never did. She bolted from the room, taking the coward's way out.

~

The orphan house was unlocked. She shouldn't have been surprised. After all, Vivien had gone back for her trunk, and she wouldn't have considered anything else in the home worth stealing, or worth protecting. Anna-Marie walked in and leaned against the door as she closed it behind her. Then, she winced. Her shoulder hurt, the flesh red and tender. Part of it had begun to knit back together, but it was clear to see she would carry a scar.

The pain gave her a direction to focus her wayward thoughts, and she took it gratefully. She pushed Lady Banks, the dragon, and her ridiculously good-humored son from her mind and set about heating water for a bath. Anna-Marie pulled a large tin tub over by the range. No sense lugging water upstairs when she was the only one here.

She allowed herself to soak, her eyelids drifting closed, playing the image of the book in her mind again. Anna-Marie considered all the possible scenarios for stealing it, even though she didn't know precisely from whom or where yet. By the time her mind and muscles had relaxed, the water was cold.

Anna-Marie dried and dressed. The quiet surrounding her seemed unfamiliar after the past week of chaos and noise. She missed the girls more than she expected and hoped Uncle Ernest had allowed Patience access to tools and books about mechanics. The girl had such an interest, much like her younger self. She also wondered how Rosie was doing. Did she feel abandoned again? Was she sad or angry? Anna-Marie reminded herself this mission was for the girls, for their future.

Even if she didn't know what that future looked like yet.

Upstairs in her old room, she cleaned all of her tinkerer's tools before wrapping them carefully back in their leather pouch. She polished her pocket watch and her red boots.

At last, she settled into bed and drifted to sleep.

Chapter Twenty-One

When Cyrus fell into step beside her the next day, Anna-Marie was unsurprised.

"Where's your puppy dog?"

"Captain Banks is seeing to his own affairs." She wouldn't let his needling get to her. Not visibly. "What's the latest on Jack of All Traders?"

"The rumor is, he's assembled a team of thieves."

"To steal more men?" She frowned.

"No." Cyrus steered them down a smaller alleyway. Once they were alone, he stopped. "To steal something from the exhibition."

Anna-Marie waited.

Cyrus studied her. "I know Ernest. I know he didn't send you here on holiday. If there's even a chance you and this Jack character are after the same thing, it puts you right in his path. Even if he's not actively hunting you, not many a man could resist revenge handed to them on a silver platter."

"Your point?"

He stepped closer, and she waited for the usual tension to settle in her stomach. It didn't. Before she could ponder that, Cyrus continued speaking.

"What are you after for Ernest?"

"It's just a book. I doubt Jack of All Traders is after a book. There will be far too many wonderful inventions and weapons available for the taking." She tried to scoot around Cyrus, but he grabbed her wrist.

He was attractive. Always had been in a dangerous way. But somehow, her desire to do something about that attractiveness had fled. Vanished. A boyish grin flitted into her mind's eye, and she blinked it away.

"Anna-Marie, I said, what book?"

"Hmm? Oh. I don't know. Some old tome with a moonstone embedded in the cover." She saw Cyrus stiffen. "What? You know it?"

"I've heard rumors of a book they call the Moonstone's Promise." He shook his head. "I don't think you want to steal that book."

"Why not?"

"I don't know what it contains. I only know the rumors are more like frightened whispers. Tales that it changes men. That it wreaks havoc. That it's promise is death." He was gripping her shoulders now. "I can get you away from Ernest. Don't do this."

"It's not just me. If I get the book, Uncle Ernest will free the girls too." She searched his gaze. "I have to do this."

"And I guess the Banks heir is going to do what you found him for. He's going to fund the orphan house and be your savior?"

"No. Only one person ever saved me, and that was you." Her chest tightened. It was true. It was one of the things that drew her like a magnet, the memory of him coming to her rescue. But she was old enough to know that a dangerous savior was still dangerous. She softened her words, begging him to understand. "But I think he's a good man, and he will try to help. If I can change things for those girls, even just a little, I have to try."

Cyrus gave a frustrated growl but let her go. "Be careful. I don't trust coincidences. This Jack of All Traders might be after an invention. But he might be after that book. I'll watch your back where I can, but I need to hit the streets and see if I can spook him out before he gets what he wants and disappears again."

"I'll be fine. Cyrus, thank you."

He nodded once, then walked away.

Anna-Marie spent the rest of the day focused on her task. She strolled the perimeter of the enormous Crystal Palace under the guise of admiring the astounding architecture of metal and glass, while she truly noted each exit and the surrounding areas.

She eyed the rooftop, much of it rounded, and discounted it as a means of entry or exit. Much too exposed and possibly none of those panels opened, anyway. She wished she'd been given more time to find the plans for the building and study them.

On her way back to the orphan house that evening, she stopped to buy a meat pie at the edge of Hyde Park.

"I thought you'd left the neighborhood for good."

She turned at the sound of the familiar voice. "Hello, Bert." She smiled. "I'm back only temporarily. What are you doing in this area?"

Bert held up his broom. "I've moved up in the world. Sweeping chimneys for the uppity houses now."

"Congratulations." She resumed walking.

"Where did all those girls you stole off with go?" He asked with a grin.

"I left them somewhere safe for now. I hope not to bring them back to the city until the man who was kidnapping them is caught."

"Caught? Are the police looking for him?"

Anna-Marie snorted. "Right. As if they care what happens to a few urchins. No, a friend of mine is looking into it."

"I see."

"Anna-Marie!"

She spun at the second voice hailing her. "Ambrose?"

"I've been looking for you." He stuck a hand out to Bert. "Hello, Ambrose Banks."

"Norbert Algernon." Bert shook hands, then turned to Anna-Marie. "I best be getting to the next house." He doffed his hat to them both.

"Friend of yours?" Ambrose asked.

Anna-Marie glanced at him, but there was no judgement, only curiosity. "Yes." She nodded. "He was a childhood friend. His father delivered coal to the orphan house, and Bert always came along. He often stayed behind until his father came back and found him, usually angry. You were looking for me?"

"That's right. I'm here to extend an invitation to dinner."

She held up her meat pie. "I'm fine, thank you. I believe your mother made her opinions of me perfectly clear."

"She wishes to…erm…apologize."

"I doubt that very much."

Ambrose chuckled. "Okay. She did promise to behave civilly. It's quite a compromise from her usual behavior."

"I'm not sure it's a good idea."

He nodded. "Of course. You're scared of her. I should have known."

"Excuse me?" She rounded on him and poked a finger in his chest. "I'm most certainly not scared of that old dragon. I could best her in a contest of insults any day, and I don't give a bloody care what she thinks of me."

It was only when she was almost finished with her outburst that she saw Ambrose trying to stifle a laugh.

"You did that on purpose," she huffed.

"So, you'll come, then?"

"Fine. But when she disinherits you for the second time, don't blame me."

Civil was a stretch. Lady Banks did not say one insulting thing. She only spoke when spoken to. And as Anna-Marie and Ambrose were perfectly content to carry on a conversation themselves, dinner was pleasant. Anna-Marie couldn't resist one tiny jab as the last course was cleared. A test of Lady Banks's word, of sorts.

"Thank you for such an exemplary meal, Lady Banks."

"You are welcome." As if it had taken all her energy to utter those three words with refined politeness, Lady Banks pled a headache and retired early.

Anna-Marie laughed. "Okay. Tell me what you agreed to in order for her to allow me to sit at her dinner table."

"What could you mean by that?"

"I can spot coercion from a block away, Ambrose. Your mother was not civil because she chose to be, but because she had something to gain by it. Let's hear it." She curled her legs beneath her on a plush cream sofa, not caring in the least if her boots got the soft fabric dirty.

Ambrose tipped his chin in acknowledgement. "You are correct. She agreed to be civil if I agreed to take on my responsibilities as the only heir."

That sucked the laughter from Anna-Marie. "She's making you give up your airship?"

Ambrose wagged a finger. "She didn't say I had to stop anything. Only that I had to do more to step into my father's shoes. Show up at public events. Accept a place in the House of Lords. Nothing about getting rid of my airship."

"Remind me not to be here when she finds out you still plan to go galivanting." She tilted her head. "On second thought, I do want to be here. I bet she breathes fire and everything."

"I'm glad my potential demise is worthy as a spectator sport."

Anna-Marie yawned. "I'd best be going."

"I'll take you round in the carriage."

She shook her head. "No, thank you. I'll walk."

"And if I insist?"

"Then, I shall insist you will be putting me in far greater danger by driving a modern and expensive steam conveyance into a neighborhood of beggars and thieves," she said as Ambrose followed her to the foyer. "I will walk, thank you."

"Fine." Ambrose collected his coat.

"What are you doing?"

"Escorting you, of course." Ambrose nodded to the butler to open the door. "If you insist on walking, then walk we shall."

"Insufferable man," she huffed as she tugged on her own overcoat.

"Ungrateful woman." Ambrose grinned unrepentantly and held out an arm.

They walked along Park Lane several blocks. Ambrose followed Anna-Marie's lead as she picked her way down side streets and shortcuts. For her part, Anna-Marie avoided the seediest alleys in order to lower the risk of Ambrose being robbed for his high-polished shoes.

Ambrose discussed his parents, what it was like growing up in the shadow of a father who bullied and harassed everyone around him, how he only disappointed the old man his whole life. Anna-Marie nodded and asked questions. It made some of her childhood longings for family less poignant, realizing family didn't always mean love or belonging. She thought of the girls, thought of the connection she had with Patience, the fondness that was growing for each of them. Perhaps, just as one could build their own tea kettle or automaton, one could build their own family as well. It was worth more thought.

At last, they came to a stop in front of Number Thirteen, Cherry Blossom Lane.

Anna-Marie ascended the steps to unlock the door, but Ambrose didn't follow. She turned to see him studying the building, his normal smile replaced by a grim frown. Her eyes perused the building as he did, and she tried to take a step back from the familiarity of it all, to see it from Ambrose's perspective.

Gray brick. The building's foundation had shifted and settled on one end. A series of small hairline cracks snaked their way up one corner, like branches extending from a tree. Dark green and black mildew reached upward along the foundation. The steps boasted an iron railing on one side only, the other long since broken and scrapped, most likely. Three of the windows had shabby, faded curtains. Two had none.

Without a word, Ambrose swept past her into the entry. She followed in silence, allowing him to inspect, to take it all in. This was what she'd wanted—someone to see the place for the dump it was, to feel accountable. It was too bad Lucifer Banks hadn't lived to be ashamed of his neglect, but from the look on his son's face, there was more than shame.

Ambrose clenched his fists as he witnessed the kitchen, the contrived bottle jack apparatus for cooking, the melted range. His nose wrinkled at the stench of smoke and stale water damage. He slammed the empty cupboard doors, ran a finger across the gouged and scratched desk in the study, and scowled at the number of beds scrunched into the attic, the mice scurrying underfoot when he opened the door.

Through it all, Anna-Marie said nothing, so when Ambrose's voice finally boomed through the quiet, she jumped.

"Get your bag."

"Pardon?"

Ambrose stalked past her to the room he'd clearly surmised was hers and snatched up the carpet bag himself. "You are not staying here another night. Do you need anything else?"

She poised herself to argue. "That is ridiculous. I've lived here most of my life, and another night or two certainly will not kill me."

"It might if I burn this place to the ground, as it deserves."

She looked for any sign of joking, of his usual devil-may-care attitude. What she saw instead was a man deadly serious. As her umbrella was still holstered on her back, she shook her head.

"I have everything I need."

"Let's go."

She didn't ask him where, only nodded. When they were several streets away from Cherry Blossom Lane, she spoke softly. "It was a roof over our heads. No matter how bad it looks, how much it was neglected by your father in the last decade, it saved many of us."

"How can you say that? How can you defend it? Defend him?"

Anna-Marie pulled him to a stop. "I'm not and never would defend him. But you didn't know. And you're berating and despising yourself, two things I will not stand for when you are not to blame."

"I should have known."

"Perhaps." Anna-Marie met his angry gaze with a steely one of her own. "Now, you do. And if your attitude is any indication, I assume you plan to do something about it, correct?"

"Bloody right. It is unconscionable that my father stood on his high horse, boasting of charity and sacrifice, while you all starved and lived in a hovel." He raked a hand through his sandy hair, mussing it wildly. "I'm going to make things right. Somehow. I promise."

"Good. Then, that's that." Anna-Marie started walking again, but strong arms pulled her back.

Ambrose spun her into his chest and hugged her. "I'm sorry," he whispered. "I'm so sorry. Thank you for making me see."

Anna-Marie wanted to relax into his warmth, stealing her own comfort as he sought his, but one hand raked her shoulder, and she winced.

Immediately, Ambrose moved away. "Forgive me."

"It wasn't that," she rushed. "It's only my shoulder. It may be infected," she admitted reluctantly.

He nodded brusquely. "Let's get home, and I'll take a look."

~

"Blazes, Anna-Marie. This is terrible. Why didn't you tell me it was hurting?" Ambrose pulled threads of fabric out of the wound where they'd become encrusted to her skin.

She shrugged. What could she say? That she'd been distracted? That pain really didn't phase her unless it slowed her down? That she wasn't sure she could be trusted to have his hands on her bare skin again?

Fortunately, Ambrose was able to fill the conversational gap, as usual. "At least none of your dresses are off of the shoulder, like the French style. Speaking of the French, I believe they and several other countries are to be represented at the exhibition. I'm particularly looking forward to the India exhibit and the great pachyderm automatons. Not as exciting as a live elephant, of course, but interesting hopefully. There are also to be some new means of predicting the weather, a useful invention if it is true."

Anna-Marie nodded. She'd heard much of the same as she scouted the location. Anna-Marie would be much more interested in the exhibits if she weren't trying to think of all the scenarios that things could go wrong and how to prevent them. She still hadn't brought Ambrose into her confidence concerning the true goal of their trip.

Anna-Marie braced herself, and Ambrose's fingers stilled. "Did that hurt too much?" he asked. "It's almost clean."

"No. I've something to tell you, actually." She tugged the large nightshirt he'd loaned her back over her shoulder. They were in his room, a fact she was pointedly ignoring.

"What is it?" Ambrose pulled a chair closer to the one she occupied in front of the fireplace.

"Uncle Ernest wants more than a meeting with the queen for me. He expects me to steal something for him. A book." She hurried to share the plan before she changed her mind.

When she finished, Ambrose stroked his chin. "What if I were to offer money to Ernest in exchange for letting you and the girls go?"

"Money means little to him. He earns gold for his inventions." She sighed. "No, if he would allow me to buy my way out, I would have scrounged and saved to do it before now. He wants this book. Badly, though I can't work out the reason why yet. Of all the things he could have asked me to do, stealing a book is a task I can live with. Then, I can put this life behind me and find some way to start fresh."

Ambrose nodded. "I don't like it, but I'll help you."

A weight lifted form her shoulders. She smiled. "Thank you. So that we understand each other, I don't like it either. However, I can live with it."

A log rolled in the fire, sending tiny embers into the air.

Ambrose cleared his throat. "Yes, well. It sounds as though we have a busy day ahead. I'll show you to your chambers."

Anna-Marie tried to convince herself the sigh she caught in her throat was relief that he was remaining the gentleman, not regret.

Chapter Twenty-Two

"It's marvelous!" Anna-Marie stared in awe at the massive mechanical beast towering above her behind the silk cords keeping people from touching it.

The India exhibit at the Great Exhibition was every bit as impressive as they had heard. The elephant waved its great gold and ivory trunk. Sculpted from precious metals and bone, with rubies studding the head and the legs, it was a work of art.

"What mysteries would you like to uncover next, Anna-Marie?" Ambrose offered his arm.

Taking it felt as natural as breathing at this point. She smiled up at him. "Why, the mysteries of our own country and monarchs, of course." She said the words jokingly, but the double meaning was clear. They had a job to do, and to do it, they needed to be noticed.

The Nave, the home of the British exhibit in the central hall of the Crystal Palace. Anna-Marie's eyes lit immediately on the largest display. She squeezed Ambrose's arm gently and turned him toward it. As they drew near, she drank in the sight of the gilded poles attached from the ornate top of the round structure, to large brass and copper ponies, unicorns, even giant fish. There was even a carriage designed and painted to match the queen's own open conveyance. She stepped closer and was shocked when the whole thing began to turn round and round. It spun faster and faster for several rotations before slowing again.

"Steam-powered roundabout," Ambrose read from the plaque.

"Would the lady care for a ticket?" A middle-aged man stepped out from behind a set of levers. "You can ride any of the animals you wish for only two shillings each."

"I'd love to!" Anna-Marie clapped her hands together.

Ambrose gave the roundabout a concerned look. "Is it safe?"

"Perfectly, my good fellow. There we are, two shillings, two shillings." The operator ushered them onto the platform of the large roundabout, and Ambrose helped Anna-Marie up on a large bronze fish, then settled himself on a pony next to her.

As the operator pulled the levers, a hiss of steam escaped beneath the ride, and then they were off. The mechanical fish moved its mouth open and shut while the hooves of the horses tilted to and fro to give the appearance of running. Anna-Marie laughed, delighted.

As the roundabout spun faster, the two had to hang on much tighter. By the time it finished, Ambrose was gripping the bar with his arms and legs, while Anna-Marie wiped tears of laughter from her eyes and slid to her bottom on the platform, too dizzy to stand on her own just yet.

It was as she turned her head to find Ambrose that she spotted a familiar coal-streaked face and black cap. Ambrose knelt to give her a hand up.

As she allowed him to tug her to her feet, she looked about but couldn't find the figure she'd glimpsed. Strange. She knew the exhibition to be open to the public, but surely Bert hadn't been afforded a day off of work to enjoy it? She shook her head. It was probably only the residual spinning of her vision making her think she saw him in the crowd of people watching the roundabout.

All thoughts of Bert vanished, when suddenly, the roundabout spun again, this time jerking into its fastest speed without warning. Ambrose and Anna-Marie were thrown sideways. They were about to slide into the center of the roundabout where the floor disappeared and the gears and wheels below turned in a blur of motion, when Ambrose saved them. He locked his knee around one of the poles holding a pony and pulled Anna-Marie against his chest.

Wildly, she searched out the operator, only to see him lying on the floor. Sparks flew from the levers, and she was afraid at any moment she and Ambrose would be shot like a cannon ball from this wild ride into the crowd of onlookers, or worse, continue their slide into the mechanisms of chomping and grinding teeth below. She narrowed her gaze at the oversized gears until she spotted what she believed to be the fulcrum.

"I need my umbrella," she called to Ambrose as she tried to wriggle one arm free from his grip.

He let go of her right arm and leaned back as she tugged the umbrella from the back of her corset. It was difficult, pressed together like this, but as their lives might well depend on it, she persevered. If Ambrose had a bruised chin from the process, he could thank her later.

"Hold my legs," she instructed next.

Ambrose only tightened his grip. "You're out of your bloody mind!"

"Trust me, Ambrose."

She felt more than heard his sigh of resignation. And then, she was sliding across the cool metal platform again as he let go, jerking to a halt when he grabbed her calves. She reminded herself to thank Madame the Hatter again for including pants in her outfit for today.

Anna-Marie counted to three and shoved her umbrella as hard as she could into the center of the whirring mechanism, then held her breath. A bone-rattling grinding noise sounded as the umbrella was wedged and bent beneath the teeth, causing them to halt. A sprocket or two flew out, and Anna-Marie ducked. The roundabout shuddered to a whining stop.

Anna-Marie released her breath in a whoosh. Suddenly, clapping sounded. The crowd cheered as Ambrose and Anna-Marie stumbled shakily from the roundabout.

The operator, rubbing his head, ran to them, stumbling over both his feet and his words as he apologized.

"I don't know what happened," he stuttered. "It was working fine. And then I felt something hit my head, and I woke up to see it spinning madly and about to break apart. Are you hurt?"

"What have we here?" A sharp, female voice sounded.

The clapping faded, and a hush fell over the crowd.

"Your Majesty!" The operator's pale skin whitened as he gulped and bowed.

Anna-Marie sunk into a belated curtsy, as all around, the crowd bowed to their monarch in some degree of awe. Apparently, they successfully had her attention.

~

"And you saw nothing that caused the machine to malfunction?" Queen Victoria gazed searchingly at Anna-Marie and Ambrose, both of whom shook their heads.

Hal, the operator, had passed out again after the queen showed up and, due to the knot on his head, was rushed to a medical tent nearby.

"No, Your Majesty," Ambrose said.

"What about someone attacking Hal, our own esteemed inventor?"

Again, two responses in the negative. A picture of a black cap flitted through Anna-Marie's head, but she ignored it, keeping her face neutral.

"While I'm grateful that you were able to stop the roundabout before it caused injury to the public, it seems we will be disgraced, as our largest exhibit is out of commission."

"Not necessarily."

"Excuse me?" The queen narrowed her eyes at Anna-Marie.

Anna-Marie straightened her spine. "I believe I can fix the roundabout. I jammed it at the fulcrum, but once the obstruction is removed and the smaller, weaker parts checked and replaced, I am confident the engine and gears will resume working without issue."

"And who are you to guarantee such an undertaking? Anna-Marie Pauper, an orphan, I presume? I've certainly never heard of you." The queen's words, though severe, were spoken with quiet curiosity as she measured the resoluteness of Anna-Marie's words with her confident posture.

"I'm the apprentice of Ernesto Rockingham." Anna-Marie easily gave the name Uncle Ernest used in his aboveboard invention business dealings.

Recognition lit the queen's features. "I see." She waved a hand at her guards, and they stepped away. "I will give you permission to work on the roundabout. It will be moved to a more private location within the hour. If you may fix it before the exhibition closes for the evening, I would be especially pleased if you and young Lord Banks would join me for a meeting this evening with several other interesting intellectuals."

"It would be our honor." Ambrose inclined his head.

"Yes, Your Majesty." Anna-Marie couldn't believe her good fortune. This task might be over sooner than she expected after all.

Chapter Twenty-Three

"Finished!" Anna-Marie wiped her hands and threw the greasy rag down in celebration. It had taken one or two threats and a few insinuations the queen would be upset if people didn't fetch her the parts she needed to get replacement springs, sprockets, and one larger gear than she'd planned to replace. It might have been exaggerating the authority Queen Victoria had actually given her over the project and the staff unfortunate enough to be in her path, but Anna-Marie didn't care.

The roundabout was fixed. In another hour, it would be returned to its rightful place in the Nave. She'd even taken the liberty of adjusting the opening width of the nozzle regulating steam. It should allow less steam to pour out at a time, thus slowing the speeds down to a somewhat more manageable, and safe, speed should anything go wrong in the future.

"You have two hours to get changed," was all Queen Victoria said when Anna-Marie informed her minutes later in the queen's private retiring chamber.

Ambrose took one look at Anna-Marie and grinned. "You're going to need every minute of those two hours." He unfolded a handkerchief from his pocket and rubbed at a spot of oil on her chin.

"For the love of tea and biscuits, it doesn't take that long to get dressed. And speaking of tea…" She tapped her pocket watch under his nose. "I believe it is time we had some."

Ambrose rolled his eyes heavenward. "I've never met a woman who is quite possibly as obsessed with taking tea as the queen herself. At least you've got that in common to discuss if you get caught tonight. 'Why was I trying to steal an ugly book from your guests? Well, Your Majesty, if you'd ring for tea, I'll gladly tell you.'"

"Poppycock. I never explain anything, tea or not."

Ambrose laughed. "I should have known."

He had the manners not to point out she had indeed explained several things to him, and Anna-Marie wouldn't have acknowledged the accusation even if he had. She smiled to herself.

The stop at the tea house was brief. Getting dressed took interminably longer than Anna-Marie anticipated, mostly because there were at least sixty buttons down the back of her scarlet dress, not counting the additional buttons of the leather corset she insisted on donning over the top. She'd eventually given up and rung for a maid to help her, which scandalized the poor girl to no end since she hadn't been informed there was a lady in the house other than Mistress Banks.

"There you are. Shall I do your hair?" the girl asked when she'd stopped hyperventilating at the prospect of being yelled at by Lady Banks for shirking her other duties to help Anna-Marie.

Anna-Marie only shrugged. "I had planned to pin it back and wear my hat."

The maid's mouth dropped open in dismay. "Not with that dress," she insisted.

With a sigh, Anna-Marie sat on the stool and handed over the hair brush. The maid said a few choice words under her breath as she brushed the tangles free, but her fingers flew swiftly and surely as she created three intricate and woven braids, which she gathered to the side and wrapped in an elegant twist. She then deftly plucked several strands free, curling them around her finger and allowing them to frame Anna-Marie's face.

With resignation, the girl also took the red hat Anna-Marie held up and placed it at a jaunty angle on top of her ebony hair, securing it with a hat pin.

"Thank you." Anna-Marie swept from the room before the maid could think of another thing to poke or prod her with, or stuff her into.

Every tedious second of effort was completely worth it when she took the first step down the staircase. Ambrose, looking up, froze and completely dropped the hat he'd been spinning on his finger.

She ran one finger along the banister as she descended. "Am I fit to be in the company of the queen?"

"I'm not sure she is fit to be in your company tonight." He whistled. "Did I tell you how delighted I was to meet Madame the Hatter? She may be one of my new favorite acquaintances."

Anna-Marie chuckled. "I'll be sure to tell her. She'll probably double the feathers in your next pirate hat with compliments like that."

"The night gets better and better." He winked.

~

"Are you certain this is the right entrance?"

"Yes." Anna-Marie nodded. "The queen's guard specifically said the westernmost rear door."

Ambrose lifted his hand to knock again. The door swung open, and his closed fist connected with the fringed shoulder of a man in uniform. "Sorry, old chap."

Without a word, the guard turned and led them through several corridors and then to another door. This door was guarded by the queen's most elite and deadly guards. Standing one and a half times the height of an average man, bulky iron and steel automatons were posted one on each side of the door. Anna-Marie, having seen designs for these monstrosities, knew that inside each one was a man piloting the intimidating machines. Designed to protect the queen from threats, human or created, they were practically indestructible. They could withstand a building being dropped on them and still bust their way through the rubble. And fighting them hand to hand? Well, Marie had a few tricks up her sleeve but two to one in this scenario would even the playing field considerably, unlike any other construct she had faced. She would prefer they avoid any scenario that involved seeing these two in action.

The first guard, the one who had led them here, slid his ring across a panel. The door opened at the sound of a tumbler rolling open. Anna-Marie and Ambrose stepped into the brightly lit room.

Unlike the elegant retiring room Anna-Marie had glimpsed earlier, this room was unadorned, aside from one long rug beneath the octagonal table in the center of the room. The walls were paneled in a light honey-colored wood, brightening the small space. The queen and five people sat at the table, which left two sides open. Anna-Marie and Ambrose took their places.

The queen nodded to the guards at the door, who left, closing it behind them.

"Allow me to introduce the newest probationary team member, Anna-Marie Pauper." Queen Victoria paused while the group at the table made no effort to conceal the way they studied Anna-Marie, as if she were a newly discovered specimen instead of an ordinary woman. Her voice rang clear as she continued. "Anna-Marie shows promising talent in the field of automaton production."

Murmurs rippled around the table.

Ambrose shifted in his seat.

"Ah, yes. Her friend, Lord Ambrose Banks."

A new voice piped up, as thin as the man from whom it came. He squinted through a pair of spectacles. "It seems there has been a Lord Banks missing from the House of Lords these last three months."

Heads swung back to Ambrose. "My father." He nodded as every pair of eyes continued to stare. "But I shall be stepping in to fill his seat forthwith?" A cross between a statement and a question, his words met with approval.

Anna-Marie relaxed as everyone nodded and went back to their own conversations. A few of those seated at the table were recognizable. Queen Victoria's Commander-in-Chief of the army sat to her left, Prince Albert to her right. The thin man with balding hair in the middle was Lord Bastion, who exerted great political influence through the House of Lords. Anna-Marie also noted the naval uniform of one of the men and assumed he was the High Admiral, though she'd never seen the man. She did know the High Admiral had a highly decorative left leg. A custom order built by Uncle Ernest when the man had lost his in an accident at sea, she had done the scrollwork of the copper sails herself and the waves were ivory tipped to give a foaming sea appearance. It was solid; any kick to that leg would harm the kicker more than the High Admiral. She made a mental note to go for his left thigh and right foot should the need to disable him arise. With the other individuals identified, that left the last man as the one carrying the book, she assumed, either with him or in his belongings.

The man had the tanned skin and fashionable headdress of the men she had seen in the India exhibit earlier that day, though his was black instead of blue or white. His clothing was also black, a loosely wrapped tunic and matching cloth pants. A single black-jeweled ring adorned his left pointer finger.

A moonstone ring, if she wasn't mistaken. Her nostrils flared. This was the target. Only a seat away from her. Being so close, she couldn't help but wonder how long her luck could hold.

And then, Queen Victoria raised her hands. Silence descended. "Some of you know why we are here today. Others may be wondering. It is my intention that nothing discussed in this room will leave it, is that clear?"

"Yes, Your Majesty," the room chorused, and Anna-Marie murmured along with the rest.

"We all know the last war will not be the last war."

More nods.

Ambrose raised an eyebrow. Anna-Marie gave a barely discernible head shake. She didn't know where this was going either.

"Raj Ahi has something that can change the destiny, our destiny, of every war to come."

It couldn't be. There was no way.

And yet.

Raj Ahi reached beneath one of the many layers of fabric making up his tunic and pulled out a thin leather tome. In the center, a fist-sized moonstone glinted black as night with thin white striations swirling from the center.

Ambrose coughed, and Anna-Marie remembered why she preferred working alone. If he didn't stop his bulging eyes from darting between her and the book, someone was going to get suspicious.

"Your Majesty, might I pour the tea?" Anna-Marie gestured to the silver tea tray in the center of the table. "I feel like it may help settle my nerves. All this discussion of war, well, I had no warning, really."

Several of the men gave affronted gasps that she would speak without being spoken to.

Instead of waiting for an answer, Anna-Marie pulled the tray toward her. Orphan. She wasn't expected to have genteel manners, and for once, she would play every low-class, ragamuffin card she'd been dealt.

Queen Victoria waved one hand with the care of someone swatting a bothersome fly and ignored her as she picked up the teapot. "While I am proud of our army and our navy, there is nothing I wouldn't do to provide our brave soldiers all of the training and weapons they need to have an edge over any other soldiers they might face."

Weapons. Anna-Marie kept her gaze focused on the tea as she listened. She allowed her hand to shake, rattling the lid. Annoyed glances flitted her way before all eyes returned to their monarch. Exactly what she'd hoped. Taking advantage, she slid a tiny satchel out of her sleeve. There was no time to measure, so she dumped a tiny bit of the powder in the teapot. Nobody turned around when the lid clinked this time.

Beside her, Ambrose also leaned forward. Brows furrowed, he looked from the queen to the book, trying to work out what she was saying. Anna-Marie didn't have time for that. They needed to get the book now and get out.

Anna-Marie filled all eight cups with tea. Quietly, murmuring false apologies and fluttering her lashes, she handed out the cups to Queen Victoria and each man at the table.

She ignored the lude comment murmured by Lord Bastion, nodded meekly to the commander as if she didn't know these men saw her as an uneducated interloper who didn't belong. If they knew how much she didn't belong, they'd do more than say rude things.

As she walked demurely back to her seat, Ambrose raised his cup to his lips and drank.

Anna-Marie gritted her teeth. She'd not had time to warn him.

Anna-Marie sat down and lifted her cup. Seeing the queen watching, she took several long, uncouth swallows.

The queen daintily sipped from her own cup, as if to show her how it was done. Taking their cue from Queen Victoria, the men at the table drank as well. Raj Ahi was last to sip. He paused to sniff his cup, and Anna-Marie praised her instincts for using a scentless sleeping herb instead of something stronger. She could feel her eyes growing tired, but long practice of exposing herself to the herbs made her ability to fight the drowsiness strong. She forced herself to remain alert as the High Admiral nodded off and Raj Ahi slurred his words, something to do with unprecedented tracking skills and enhanced speed.

She tucked two fingers into an interior pocket and plucked a capsule out. Ambrose looked at her with a goofy smile. He was about to fall into the deep slumber. She had only seconds to prevent it, but only one capsule of liquid antidote, and she didn't dare risk breaking it and spilling a single drop.

Anna-Marie did the only thing she could think of. Throwing the capsule in her mouth, she bit down to break it, then grabbed Ambrose around the neck and kissed him hard on the mouth. She tipped it open with her tongue, spilling as close to half the liquid as she could estimate into his mouth.

When she let go, the stupor he went into wasn't from the herbs, and she couldn't help the tiny, wicked smile as he stared at her in shock.

"Snip, snap." She winked as she grabbed the book. "We have to get out of here before they wake up. We only have two hours, give or take."

"What was that? And what do you mean, give or take?" Ambrose blinked hard, stumbling slightly as he jumped to his feet.

She shrugged. "I couldn't exactly pull out a spoon and measure an exact amount of sleeping herbs per person's cup, now could I? Depending on the dose, they may sleep less or more."

"Great. So not only was Cyrus right about a spoonful of anything being dangerous with you, but evidently, you're dangerous without even a spoon around to blame."

"Are you more dismayed that I drugged you, or that Cyrus was right about me?" she whispered over her shoulder, listening at the door for signs of the guards.

"That Cyrus was correct, of course. If that kiss was any indication of your apologies for drugging me, you can muddle up my tea any time."

"Apology? That wasn't an apology. I simply wanted you to have enough antidote that I didn't have to lug your unconscious form out of here. My good umbrella was eaten by a roundabout, if you recall, so flying out isn't exactly an option."

"I see," Ambrose whispered. "What are we doing?"

"Hoping the guards go away?"

"Have they?"

She stood up and moved back. "No. I can hear them talking. Rooms like this always have secret doors. Start pulling on sconces or pressing on panels."

"I think that finding a secret room might take longer than just knocking out the guards and running for our lives," Ambrose muttered. Nevertheless, he began diligently pressing both hands at intervals along the walls.

Anna-Marie paused to pass a studied eye around the sparse room once more.

There.

A lone knothole on the back wall.

Tucking the book under her arm, she sprinted to the knothole. "Ambrose, bring me your hat."

"My hat?" He brought the pirate hat with a frown.

Anna-Marie tugged the feather fitted with the needle-like sword out of the band. She stuck the tip into the hole in the wall and slowly moved it right to left, left to right. When she moved it down to up, the panel whooshed open.

"Thank you!" She grinned as she poked the feather hastily back into the hat.

Following behind her, Ambrose muttered under his breath about women and trouble and hats. Anna-Marie was listening for other noises. She clung to the shadows, glancing back only long enough to ascertain Ambrose was doing the same. As far as she could discern, no guards patrolled this hall. They were back in a portion of the Crystal Palace walled with glass panels. Anna-Marie looked outside, but the torches still lit inside reflected off the glass, making it impossible to see out. She wouldn't be able to gain her bearings that way.

"Do you know where we are?" she asked when Ambrose caught up.

He squinted. "As a matter of fact, no."

She sighed. "I'll be right back."

Slipping the book beneath her corset, she sprinted silently on her toes to the next booth and shimmied up the curtain. The upper balconies were dark. She crept to the wall and peered out. The fog was thick, and the moon hid behind a cloud, but she could tell by the lack of structures jutting into the air, they were somewhere on the front side of the building, facing Hyde Park.

"There should be a door in the center of this wall. We'll have to go behind the booths to find it," she whispered.

Ambrose began to reply, then jerked her on the other side of the column. "Shh," he whispered, so low it was barely audible, even so close to her ear.

Another noise sounded from the booth behind them. They froze.

Then, a long, loud snore drifted through the air, and they covered their mouths to stop their laughter.

"False alarm," Ambrose whispered.

The two tiptoed carefully between statues, plants, and closed food stands. At last, Anna-Marie spotted what she was looking for—a long bar across one panel of glass. The handle for the door.

She pointed and Ambrose nodded. He stepped in front and opened it, looking out. Signaling the coast to be clear, he opened it for Anna-Marie and shut it softly behind them.

For the first hundred yards, they sprinted from tree to bush, not risking the slightest chance of being spotted. Once they exited Hyde Park, Anna-Marie quickened their pace.

It had all been far too easy. She could taste her freedom. And life had taught her well. Good things are never easy.

"We're almost there," Ambrose said. "It's a nice night for a moonlit stroll. Do you think it's safe to slow down?"

"No."

"Okay…" Ambrose matched her hurried pace easily with his long strides. He looked back and around. "I don't see anyone following us. Racing along the streets in the middle of the night is sure to be more suspicious than walking at a normal pace."

"What's the matter, Captain Banks? Can't keep up?"

Ambrose reached for her, but Anna-Marie danced away from him. "Come back here."

As if they hadn't just stolen classified and likely dangerous intel from a foreign dignitary under the nose of the queen, or maybe because that is exactly what they had done, the two raced on. Anna-Marie slowed until Ambrose nearly caught her before changing directions.

The third time she did it, he was ready for her. Ambrose feinted right and spun to catch her as she tried to double back to his left.

"I told you I would catch you," he whispered.

Anna-Marie shivered. "It's a shame for you that we didn't make a wager then, isn't it?"

"How do you know I didn't wager with myself?"

Anna-Marie tapped her chin. "That does seem like something you might do, seeing as how it is utterly ridiculous."

Ambrose caught her hand before she lowered it to her side. "Precisely. Would you like to know what I've won?"

"I am not at all sure that would be wise."

Ambrose leaned down. "I'll tell you anyway."

"Yes?"

He moved until his lips were nearly to her own. Then, he whispered, "I plan to help Madame the Hatter design your next hat."

"What?" Anna-Marie gasped.

"Oh, yes. I can see a bright yellow monstrosity in your future. Like a canary. No! With a canary on it, in the hideous fashion that is rearing its head these days." Ambrose extolled the ludicrous plans for a hat with glee.

"Men!" Anna-Marie stomped ahead of him, doubling her breakneck pace.

She went all of ten steps before Ambrose tucked her arm into his own. "Don't you like the hat idea? Wait. Don't tell me, you thought I would say I won a kiss."

The insufferable man was baiting her. She refused to give him the satisfaction of an answer. As if her silence phased him a bit.

"Don't you remember? I promised that when you kiss me, it will be because you've fallen for me." They arrived outside of his mother's townhouse. "And say what you will about poison tea and antidotes, but you could have left me asleep in that room and gotten away, free as a bird."

"That is only because I couldn't trust you not to break under torture." Anna-Marie stomped on his foot as she moved past him toward the steps.

If she had been less flustered, she might have noticed the shadow detaching itself from the side of the house. If she'd not been out of breath—from running, of course, not from the absurd conversation—she would have reacted faster.

Instead, she stood stock still and shook her head as the shadow stepped under the gas light. Ambrose turned to see what she was looking at.

"Evening gov'," the man said, as he hit Ambrose square in the side of the head.

Chapter Twenty-Four

"Bert." Anna-Marie took a step back. The hat she'd seen in the Nave, the sooty face, it hadn't been her imagination. "Norbert Jack Algernon." She said the name slowly. Her lips curled as if it left a bad taste in her mouth. "Jack of All Traders. Tell me it isn't so. It can't be."

"Why can't it be? Poor Bert, too poor and stupid to make anything of himself, is that it?" Bert stalked closer.

Anna-Marie thought she might be able to outrun him, but she couldn't leave Ambrose out cold on the sidewalk at his mercy.

He sneered. "Not even worth your time to say goodbye. I tried to give you another chance. We could have been together. But you chose all of those brats over me and then went and threw yourself at the first wealthy gent that gave you the time of day."

"No, I meant it couldn't be possible that my friend Bert, the boy who grew up in the slums and knew just how hard life was for children like us, chose to grow up and victimize them further." Anna-Marie tucked the book tighter beneath her arm. "What are you going to do with this, anyway?"

"The same thing the queen wanted to do with it. Build an army."

Bert whistled. Three more men dressed as chimney sweeps materialized in the street.

Four-to-one weren't impossible odds, especially for Anna-Marie. Still, Uncle Ernest's training was about to be tested. She couldn't put down the book and let Bert get to it, so she did the only thing possible—shoved it between her corset and her dress. Thank goodness it wasn't some three-inch thick manual of procedures.

With her hands free, she pulled a short sword from each boot.

The chimney sweeps all twisted their broomsticks, which came apart to reveal wicked-looking blades of their own.

Lovely.

Bert clapped his hands, and so the dance began.

All three men charged her at once. She waited until she could hear the swish of their sticks in the air before she ducked and launched herself between the first and second man. She sliced their calf muscles, leaping away and back up. One limped around to find her, while the other stayed on the ground, cradling his leg.

The third man hurled his sword stick like a spear. Anna-Marie jumped to the side.

"Don't damage the book!" Bert whispered a harsh command.

The men changed aim, jabbing and slicing at her legs. She leaped and twirled. One knife slid right through the split in her skirts. She jerked the stick and kicked the man in the face.

The last man grabbed her from behind, and she snarled as fiercely as any caged animal. With one, two, three kicks backward with the blade on her heel, she left the man with more holes in his leg than a good Swiss cheese.

"Bravo, bravo." Bert clapped. He straightened from the light pole where he'd been watching and walked toward her.

"Your turn, is it?" she asked.

"It is, but I'm not going to fight you."

Anna-Marie laughed. "If you think I'll hand over the book because you say please, you will be sorely disappointed." She brought both arms up in a defensive position, watching for his first move.

"I was afraid you'd say that. Lucky for me, I stopped by to see dear Uncle Ernest."

Anna-Marie's heart sped up. If he had been to Foxhold Manor…the girls! "What did you do?" she hissed.

"We had a chat, and I borrowed a few things, that's all. Like this tiny little dart."

Anna-Marie's eyes widened. She spun, but it was too late. The poison blow dart embedded itself in her shoulder, and she collapsed on Lady Banks's grassy lawn. Temporarily paralyzed, she was forced to watch as Bert knelt over her. He ran both hands over the bottom of her corset before slipping them beneath and pulling out the book.

And there was nothing she could do about it.

Her eyes wouldn't obey her commands enough to even glare.

"Goodbye, sweet Anna-Marie."

Chapter Twenty-Five

Anna-Marie practically knocked the door off the hinges as she burst into Foxhold Manor two days later.

Once she and Ambrose had both come to, it had been too late to take the train. By the next day, she'd had enough time to think. Queen Victoria would be hunting them. They couldn't just waltz to the train station and buy a ticket with every copper in the city having been programmed to recognize them. Ambrose, too, insisted he couldn't leave right away. He secreted himself in the study with a trusted steward. She assumed he was getting affairs in order for his mother, in case of the worst, and didn't press him.

Madame the Hatter had disguises. Even Ambrose wasn't surprised this time, though he was less than pleased to be dressed as an elderly scholar. Anna-Marie transitioned seamlessly into her own role as a meek and dutiful servant. Even with all of her agitation and impatience boiling her insides, the calm veneer that had been her shield for most of her life was firmly in place once more.

"Patience! Rosie, Temperance! Vivien!" She yelled for the girls.

And miracle of miracles, they all came running down the stairs.

"Anna-Marie, you're back!" Temperance threw her arms around Anna-Marie's waist.

Ambrose's look of relief matched her own when he saw the girls were unharmed, all of them. Only one was missing.

"Prudence, can you take the girls to the lake? I think it is a lovely day for a picnic."

"Absolutely!"

As the girls ran giggling for the back terrace and the lake, Anna-Marie pulled Patience aside. "Where is Vivien?"

"In her room, I guess. She hasn't really come out much since Bert visited."

"Visited?" She tried to hide the anxiety in her voice. Merely a polite inquiry.

Ambrose stepped closer, a steadying presence.

"Yes, he came to…Well, I don't think he ever said why he came." Patience shrugged. "I think maybe he was the fellow that Vivien was sneaking out to see all of the time."

"I think maybe you're right," Anna-Marie murmured.

"Oh! One more thing."

"Yes?"

Patience pulled a small blinking device from her apron pocket. "I found this on Constantina, stuck to the inside of that little door, but I didn't remember it being there when you showed me how to work on her. I couldn't find anywhere that it fit, so I took it out."

"Thank you, Patience."

Squeals sounded outside, and the young woman went to help her sister with the other girls.

"Vivien?" Ambrose asked.

Anna-Marie waved away the question. "No. She can wait. I need to see something first." Even as she walked beneath the stairs and pulled the sconce on the wall, she had a strange empty feeling in her stomach.

Ambrose didn't speak. He stepped onto the secret platform beside her, placing a hand at the small of her back to provide the support she hadn't asked for. Support she hadn't even realized she needed until the door opened into the workshop and she saw the awful scene she'd been dreading.

Uncle Ernest hung limply from the rack above his work area. He had been tortured.

Anna-Marie turned away, refusing to look for all the details in the scene that would replay his last hours for her. "I can't," she gulped.

"I'll take care of it. Go downstairs and be with the girls."

She spent hours outside, chatting and laughing, even when her heart wasn't in it. On one hand, she was free. The girls were free. On the other hand, she was a fugitive, and they were trapped in this life of very little choices, the same as they had been. The scenery was just prettier now.

Ambrose joined them eventually. He gave her a swift nod to let her know the body had been taken care of.

She excused herself to go make the picnic. The girls told her all of the staff had gone on holiday.

Instead of going to the kitchen, she walked upstairs. Vivien's room was empty, and her trunk was gone. That combined with the tiny location telegraphing device Patience had found attached to Constantina was all the proof she needed.

Vivien and Bert had planned this from the beginning, and somehow, she'd missed it.

Back downstairs, she collected cheese and grapes and a soft loaf of bread. As she placed everything into a basket, two strong hands settled on her shoulders, thumbs making circles. Ambrose carefully avoided her wound, which had finally closed up and stopped draining.

"I'm sorry, Anna-Marie."

"It's so silly of me. He wasn't my real uncle. I'm finally free of his influence, his missions.

There's no reason I should mourn him. It isn't practical." She sniffed.

"No, it's not." He turned her gently to face him. "But as practical as you try to be, you aren't one of those automatons with practical programming. You are human. And that's a perfectly perfect thing to be." He kissed her forehead.

Anna-Marie smiled, a wobbly smile. She wiped her eyes. "I'll be human later. Right now, let's not spoil the mood for the girls. I do hate that they won't get the education in reading and writing, cooking and tinkering that Foxhold Manor could have afforded."

"I've been meaning to talk to you about that," he said, holding the door open for her.

"Oh?" She tipped her chin up and raised a hand to block the afternoon sunshine from her eyes as she studied him.

"Food!" Rosie's yell set a chorus of cheers ablaze across the grassy meadow.

Soon, thundering footsteps were headed their way.

Ambrose only grinned. "Sounds like it will have to wait. Let's feed these little ragamuffins and enjoy this bit of freedom while it is ours to enjoy."

To be continued….

Anna-Marie and Ambrose's story to continue in book 2, *A Spoonful of Madness*, as they embark on a mission to retrieve the stolen book, *Moonstone's Promise*

Other Fiction Books by Katherine Brown

Sassy Supplies Cozy Mystery Series:

Costumes & Cadavers

Turkeys & Tragedy

Gingerbread & Gravediggers

Hearts & Hostages

Pinches & Peril

Bunnies & Burglaries

Serape & Scapegoats

Fireworks & Fraud

Ooey Gooey Bakery Mystery Series:

Rest, Relax, Run for Your Life

Pastries, Pies, & Poison

Bake, Eat, & Be Buried

Savory, Sweet, & Scandalous

Couches & Catastrophes (Book 3.5)

Red Velvet & Romance (Book 4.5) A Valentine's Short

White Chocolate, Weapons, & a Walk Down the Aisle (Book 5)

Young Adult/Fantasy Romantic Mystery & Adventure

The Librarian's Treasure

Children's Books

Princess Bethani's First Garden Party

Princess Bethani's Surprise Visitor

Ghost Boy Camps Out

Becky Beats the Mean Girls

Adventures of Gladys (Ooey Gooey Spinoff Series)

Bonbon Voyage

Half-Baked Homecoming

Non-Fiction / Gift Books by Katherine Brown

Books for Mom

Being a BONUS Mom is…

Being a Mom is… (A little Book of Big Laughs)

Books for Teens & Women

Just a Girl, Dreaming of a Wedding (A Faith-Filled Wedding Planning Journal) available in four styles below:

Pineapple Cover

Red Roses Cover

White Lace Cover

Rose Gold Glitter Cover

www.ingramcontent.com/pod-product-compliance
Lightning Source LLC
LaVergne TN
LVHW041218080526
838199LV00082B/778